Seeing Each Other

Their eyes met and Brenda felt a little self-conscious. She started to shake the snow out of her hair. He watched her.

"Do you feel better? You're not dizzy or anything, are you?"

"No. I'm fine."

"You look okay. Actually you look better than okay." He now had a soft look in his eyes that sent a tingle all the way through her.

"Yeah, sure." Brenda laughed. She retied her bandana and emptied the caked snow that was wedged in the cuffs of her jeans.

"How about a ski lesson?" Brad suggested suddenly.

Brenda hesitated, "Well. . . ."

"It can't be any worse than what just happened."

"I guess I could use a lesson."

"There's an intermediate slope on the other side. Do you want to try that?"

Brenda nodded.

"Go on ahead of me," Brad said warmly. "I'll be right behind you if you fall."

Books from Scholastic
in the Couples series:

ALONE, TOGETHER

Linda A. Cooney

SCHOLASTIC INC.
New York Toronto London Auckland Sydney

ISBN 0-590-33392-5

12 11 10 9 8 7 6 5 4   6 7 8 9/8 0/9

Printed in the U.S.A.   06

ALONE, TOGETHER

Chapter
1

"**B**renda!"

Brenda Austin slammed her locker door shut at the sound of her stepsister's voice. The corridor was a mass of frantic bodies in parkas and plastic raincoats, all fighting one another to beat the third period tardy bell. Brenda saw tall, blond Chris weaving toward her and immediately began walking in the opposite direction. She didn't care where she might end up — all she wanted was to avoid her stepsister.

"Brenda, wait up!" Chris yelled. Her voice was now insistent and very loud.

Brenda continued to walk away. She was headed for the main entrance of Kennedy High — the opposite direction of her third period Spanish class. But as Brenda rushed around the corner, she found herself facing the point of a freshman's umbrella. She hesitated for a moment, and that was all it took for Chris to catch up. The touch of her stepsister's hand on her arm caused Brenda to pull away.

"Hi," Chris offered, panting slightly.

"Hi," Brenda responded tersely.

Chris swung her long blond hair so that it lay neatly against the back of her navy blazer. Chris looked every inch the homecoming princess, honor student, and all-American beauty that she was. Just looking at Chris always made Brenda feel that she had been born on the wrong planet.

"You dropped one of your gloves." Chris smiled, holding out a black glove that was cut off at the fingertips. She offered it to Brenda.

"Oh. Thanks." Brenda started to walk again, and Chris followed.

"Brenda, can I talk to you for a second?"

"Sure."

"Well, not if you keep walking so fast."

Brenda stopped and faced Chris. She stuck her hands in the pockets of her jean jacket and threw her weight to one hip. She might stop walking, but she wouldn't necessarily listen to whatever Chris had to say. Brenda looked down at her wrist and played with her slim rhinestone bracelet.

"Are you going to that assembly fourth period?" Chris asked.

"That music thing?" Brenda sighed with mock boredom and pushed back her dark, wispy hair.

"It's a harpsichordist. It should be really good."

"The whole junior class has to be there, so I guess I'm going."

"Oh, right. Well, I thought I'd save you a seat; you know, so you could sit with me and Ted." Chris was smiling sweetly at Brenda. "Come on,

Bren. Phoebe and Woody are going to sit with us."

Before Brenda knew it she was walking again. It was a reflex. The mention of Phoebe or Woody, or any of Chris's popular friends, made Brenda want to fly away. How was it possible for a girl who had run away from home, who didn't get great grades, didn't have many friends — how could Chris imagine that Brenda could even hope to compete against people like Chris and her friends? It was hopeless. Brenda frowned as she gained speed and passed the trophy case in the front hallway. She was headed for the main entrance. Chris stayed with her until Brenda reached the doorway.

"I'd rather sit by myself, thanks." Brenda pushed through the double doors.

"Brenda," Chris called after her as the third period bell rang out, "don't you have Spanish now? Where are you . . . ?"

Brenda was out in front of the school before Chris had finished her sentence. The rain had stopped, but the air was still thick and damp. Tiny puddles covered the uneven asphalt of the parking lot, and Brenda skirted around them, holding her notebook against her chest like a shield. She knew she wasn't supposed to be out there — the area was off limits during class — but Brenda would have gone anywhere to escape Chris and her friends. What made Chris think that people would accept Brenda so easily? Brenda knew what would happen. She would just be suspected and snubbed — again.

The tardy bell rang as Brenda walked over a tiny knoll that bordered a far section of the parking lot. It was hard to see this area from the main office window. The first thing Brenda noticed when she looked up was a car full of kids, slumped down and passing cigarettes back and forth. One of them — a boy with stringy blond hair — popped up over the dashboard and waved a long arm. "Hey," he called softly, "want a smoke?"

Brenda instinctively turned and walked the other way. She knew she wanted no part of that loser crowd. She didn't know what crowd she *did* want to belong to. All the cliques and groups at Kennedy seemed artificial. It was as though everyone had everyone else pegged — you had to belong to this group or that. Chris didn't seem so concerned with social rules, but she belonged to the most popular group of all. She couldn't know what it was like.

"Hey!"

Brenda froze. She recognized the voice instantly. Slowly she looked back to see Mr. Aldino, one of the school monitors, rushing in her direction. He hadn't spotted the car where Brenda had seen the kids smoking, but he had seen her.

"Hey!" Mr. Aldino yelled once more. "What are you doing out here?"

Brenda shook her head. She hadn't intended to cut class. Why did he have to catch her? Somehow everything she did turned into some kind of a mess. She couldn't explain to Mr. Aldino that she just wanted to think for a few minutes. She was going to go to Spanish class. She really was.

"Austin?" Mr. Aldino's voice was tainted with disappointment as he recognized her. He shook his head and his tweed hat wobbled from side to

4

side. "I haven't caught you cutting since last year." He gave her a sad, fatherly look. "I thought you were doing okay now. What is this junk you're pulling? You kids are giving me gray hairs."

"I was just going to class."

"Do you have a pass?"

"No, but —"

Mr. Aldino raised his hand, and Brenda knew instantly it wasn't any use to protest. He wasn't interested in her explanation. He had caught Brenda off campus and she was going to the vice-principal's offce.

"Okay," Mr. Aldino said, "let's go."

Brenda huffed and followed him toward the main office. She tried to stay cool. This was the first time she'd been in any trouble at school since she ran away. At least they wouldn't call her step-father this time; that punishment only came after being caught three times in one semester.

"Get a late slip," Mr. Aldino said as he led her into the eleventh-grade office. He made a sad, clucking sound, tipped his hat, and went back toward the parking lot.

There were already two other girls sitting in the chairs waiting to talk to Mrs. Godwin, the eleventh-grade vice-principal. That meant Brenda would probably have to wait another ten minutes, which would make her even later. Then she'd have to walk into Spanish class with the slip and present it to Ms. Shireson. Everybody there would know she'd been caught and sent to the office. All this because she had simply wanted to be left alone.

Brenda sat down in the folding chair nearest the window and tried to figure out how things had gotten so out of control. Suddenly the girl next to her leaned toward her.

"That guy out there is waving at you."

Brenda glanced up. It was Ted Mason — Chris's boyfriend. He looked quizzically at Brenda, motioning to her in some kind of sign language. The girl next to Brenda giggled, but she felt like hiding her face in her hands. Ted was okay — nicer to Brenda than most of the popular kids at Kennedy — but his seeing her there could only make things worse. Now her trip to the office would get back to Chris and then to her folks. Brenda would have to offer a lame excuse for her behavior, and she'd be punished and embarrassed.

Ted finally waved and took off down the corridor. The heavily made-up girl next to Brenda smiled. "Boy, that guy is cute," she said. "Isn't he on the football team or something?"

Brenda nodded.

"Is he your boyfriend?"

Brenda shook her head and almost laughed; the girl's question was ludicrous. But she felt too miserable to laugh. She pressed the palms of her hands against her closed eyes and tried to pretend that she wasn't really sitting in the vice-principal's office, that she was someplace else and everything was okay.

It was no use. When she opened her eyes she was still on the same green vinyl couch, waiting to go into the office. Another disaster, Brenda admitted to herself. They just kept on coming.

"She was in Godwin's office last period? Oh no. It's all my fault."

"Chris, how can it be your fault? Brenda was the one in the office."

Chris let her forehead fall against Ted's chest and took a deep breath. They were on their way to the fourth period music assembly, but had ducked under the second story stairwell for a few moments of semi-quiet.

"Because I wanted her to sit with us at the assembly, and she got freaked and ran off. Just what she needs — to get in trouble for cutting again. My dad will have a fit."

Chris felt Ted's arms wrap protectively around her. For a moment she leaned against him and was soothed by the slick leather of his letterman's jacket against her cheek. She was frustrated and worried, and on top of that she had the chills. Slipping her arms around Ted's waist, she held him tightly until she began to feel better.

"Hey." Ted stroked the back of her hair. "Are you okay?"

Chris smiled. No, she wasn't okay, but being with Ted made everything seem a little less dire. "I think I'm getting a cold." She sniffed and pulled back to look Ted in the face. "It just makes me crazy! Why won't Brenda do anything with us at school? It would be so good for her."

Ted grinned at her. "Okay, Mom."

"What's that supposed to mean?"

He winked at her and led her back into the corridor and down the hallway. People rushed past, hurrying to get good seats for the assembly. When Ted and Chris reached the bottom of the stairs, Ted suddenly stopped and gently held Chris's shoulders. "I just mean that it's her life.

7

You can't make her do something if she really doesn't want to."

"I know."

In front of the passing crowd, Chris hugged Ted again. Chris remembered a time when she wouldn't have dreamed of hugging Ted in front of her classmates, when she would have been too worried about behaving properly. But she had changed, softened, loosened up. If she could change, so could Brenda.

Chris relaxed her embrace and the two walked toward the auditorium. People were bottled up at the double-door entrance and now spilled into the hall. "I never should have run for homecoming princess," Chris muttered as they waited for the crowd to thin out, still thinking about Brenda and her determined isolation.

"Chris, give yourself a break," Ted whispered back. He stood on his tiptoes to see over the top of the crowd and ran a hand through his curly hair.

Chris sighed. She had been elected homecoming princess, but only after a rugged campaign that included a lot of vicious gossip about Brenda by Laurie Bennington, who tried to ruin Chris's chances. Some of it had gone out over WKND, the Kennedy High radio station. It made Chris furious to think that Brenda, who was so vulnerable, had been used in that way. Chris emerged from the whole mess with the homecoming crown, while Brenda won another blow to her self-esteem.

Chris felt guilty, even though she knew it wasn't really her fault. She wanted to make it up to her stepsister. Under Brenda's sullen exterior was someone very special. Chris had seen glimpses of her and wanted to encourage that side of her stepsister. She wanted the whole school to see it. Maybe then Brenda would see it.

"Don't blame yourself," Ted added as they slowly moved forward. "It's not your fault if she wants to be mad at the world. All you can do is keep trying to help her."

Chris smiled and kept a firm hold on Ted's hand.

"Hey, what is this assembly thing anyway?" he demanded. "If it's as boring as that opera singer we had last time, don't expect me to be on good behavior. Hearing those high notes just does something to me."

"I'm sure you can control yourself," Chris teased back, with a jab at Ted's ribs. "Come on."

The foyer was crowded wall to wall, but Ted and Chris moved steadily ahead. As first string quarterback, Ted had a great talent for weaving through crowds. Chris was glad he had taken charge. She was still preoccupied with Brenda and was starting to feel chilled and tired again.

Inside the auditorium, Chris spotted Phoebe Hall, her best friend, and pulled Ted in Phoebe's direction. She was standing at the edge of the aisle waving, her full red hair in a mass of loose curls around her face. She was wearing a typical Phoebe outfit — denim culottes and a funky green cardigan over a man's shirt and tie. Farther in sat Woody Webster, carefully guarding three empty seats, and Sasha Jenkins, who was scribbling in a small notebook.

"Are we late?" Chris asked as she gave Phoebe

a hug. Chris squeezed past Phoebe to the middle of the row. Ted followed and sat down just as the tardy bell rang.

"Just in the nick," joked Woody, one thumb in his red suspenders. "But I don't think they're going to start for a little while. The PA system is on the blink. Peter's up there trying to fix it." Woody craned his neck and pointed to Peter Lacey, another member of the crowd who was up on stage examining the microphone. Peter backed away from the microphone and ran a hand through his dark, wavy hair. He wore a black T-shirt that advertised WKND where he served as chief deejay.

"I've told the stage crew class that it's been a little weird lately, but do they pay attention to me?" Woody laughed.

"Well, I'm glad we have to wait," added Sasha, scratching the base of her dark braid with the end of her pencil. "I'm supposed to review this concert for the newspaper, plus I have this big essay due next Monday for Barnes's English class." She wrinkled her nose, the translucent skin showing just a hint of color. "Plus the ski trip tomorrow." Chris had almost forgotten the school ski trip that most of the crowd had signed up for. "I need every extra second I can get."

Woody poked Sasha with his elbow. "Sash, you need more wheat germ, more bran."

Sasha tapped his knee with her pencil. She was the original health-food fanatic and Woody loved to tease her about her obsession. "Bran is not for energy, Woody." She paused. "But I do think I may be eating too much sugar."

They all laughed. Chris looked at her friends' warm and lively faces. They were all accomplished, original. Woody directed the school follies and most other dramatic productions. His expressive features were always filled with energy and humor. Loyal, predictably flaky Sasha was the best writer on the school newspaper. Peter's funny, charming radio personality complimented his caring and thoughtful attitude toward his friends, and Phoebe, down at the other end of the row, was the warmest, most giving friend Chris had ever known. And Ted, of course, kept Chris laughing, loved her, and reminded her not to take life so seriously.

It was a wonderful group of friends, one that Chris couldn't have lived without. Yet Brenda insisted on isolating herself from them. Chris's friends weren't snobs. They were all willing to give Brenda a chance, if only Chris could get Brenda to give herself one.

Chris twisted in her seat and searched the auditorium for her stepsister. Kids were half-standing, half-kneeling, or bent over the backs of chairs — it was almost impossible to find anyone. Surveying the audience, Chris spotted Janie Barstow, a tall, shy girl from the school radio station, sitting toward the back and straining to see the stage. Chris tried to wave, but Janie was watching the stage so intently that she didn't see the gesture. Chris continued to look for Brenda. She had just found her in an aisle seat on the opposite side when Ted tugged the sleeve of her sweater.

"It's our fearless leader," Ted joked warmly, gesturing to the front.

Chris sat up straight as a sandy-haired boy strode confidently out to the center of the stage. He held his arms up to get everyone's attention, but he didn't even need to. As student body president he was at ease in front of them all and well-known as a leader at school — he only had to appear for the crowd to hush up. Brad Davidson stood broad-shouldered and tall in khaki slacks and a pressed blue shirt. Still a good friend of Ted's, Brad had been very close to Chris when he was Phoebe's boyfriend. But since he and Phoebe had broken up he had been keeping his distance.

Brad walked up to the very edge of the stage and smiled easily. Cupping his hands over his mouth to form a natural megaphone, he spoke to the junior class.

"As you can see, we have a problem up here. We have our best technical experts working on it." Peter held up a posed bicep and Brad smiled. "And we know you're all glad to be out of class anyway." Everybody laughed. "So, if you'll all just hold tight and keep the noise down, we'll get this going as soon as we can." Brad waved and walked purposefully off the stage. There was light applause and the audience went back to a low level of chatter.

As Brad climbed down from the stage, Ted bobbed up to wave him over, motioning that there was a waiting seat. Brad smiled and began to walk across the auditorium to join the group. His strong face was open and warm until he spotted Phoebe at the end of the row. As soon as Brad saw his ex-girlfriend, his face turned to stone and his walk stiffened. With an abrupt turn he changed direction and walked to a seat on the other side of the auditorium.

Ted sunk in his seat and whispered to Chris, "Can you believe he still won't sit with us if Phoebe's around? He's getting to be a real case."

Chris strained her neck to see where Brad had gone. She could just catch his profile. He was sitting on the end of the last row looking angrily in front of him. One of the most popular guys in the school was acting as weird as Brenda. He had been moody ever since Phoebe ended their two-year relationship.

"How's Brad doing?" Chris asked. A couple of months earlier, Brad had called her almost as often as he called Ted. Now Chris couldn't remember when they had last spoken.

Ted wrapped his arms over his chest and whispered, "He's burying himself under his college applications and student government projects. Still *Mr. Leader*, Princeton-bound and all, but inside he's a mess. You know what happened when I tried to fix him up with my cousin."

Chris nodded and leaned her head on Ted's shoulder. Ted had tried to introduce Brad to his attractive cousin who was a senior at a nearby private school, but Brad virtually ignored her when they met at a downtown dance club. Since Phoebe had left him for Griffin Neill, Brad seemed afraid to begin dating anybody else.

Ted leaned toward Chris again. "He won't admit it, but I think he's just paranoid he's going to get hurt again. He's pretty angry all the time, or maybe he's just scared. It's a real drag. I hate to say it, but you know who he reminds me of?"

"Who?"

Ted pointed over to the other side of the auditorium. There was Brenda sitting in an end seat, leaning forward with her chin in her hands. Her layered hair hid her face, but her posture advertised her defensiveness and hostility.

The buzz of feedback from the microphone and a rousing cheer in the auditorium brought Chris's attention back to the stage. Peter bowed and scurried off the stage as the house lights dimmed. After a few whistles and catcalls, the audience gradually grew quiet.

"Ted," Chris whispered.

He leaned his ear close to her mouth, keeping his eyes on the stage. "Hmm?"

"I wonder if you're right."

"I usually am." He flashed a mischievous grin. "About what?"

"About Brad being scared."

"Maybe."

"And about that being Brenda's problem, too."

"Could be." The lights had come up on the stage and Ted was straining his neck to see the harpsichord. He let out a tiny laugh. "It's like a piano that went in the dryer."

Chris lightly slapped his arm. "I just never thought about it that way, that she was scared."

Ted patted her hand and held a silencing finger to his lips.

A spotlight focused on the microphone and Principal Beaman stepped in to introduce the guest musician. But Chris was still thinking about Brenda. It just might be true that she was afraid to become a part of Kennedy High. If Brenda really was scared, Chris had an idea how to break through. She'd have to wait for the right opportunity, but maybe it would work.

A note from the harpsichord floated through the auditorium, and Chris began to smile.

Chapter 2

"What happened in school today, girls?"

Brenda's head snapped up and her fork dropped. With a tinny ring it bounced off the china plate and onto her lap.

"Nothing," Brenda answered her stepfather as she picked up her fork and laid it on the tablecloth.

Chris was sitting across the table, but didn't say anything. Brenda could tell Chris was thinking about something serious — she was pushing her food aimlessly around her plate. Nervously wondering if Chris was going to mention the trouble during third period, Brenda cleared her throat and stared at her plate.

"What do you mean, nothing? How can anyone do nothing all day?" Mr. Austin asked with a smile.

Brenda held back. It was his standard comeback to Brenda's standard answer. At least he said it with humor now, not with the disapproving scowl he had given Brenda so often in the past. But Brenda didn't know what to say. All she could think about was how she'd spent half of Spanish class in the eleventh-grade vice-principal's office.

"Um," Brenda began, "I guess that —"

"Brenda and I went to this great music assembly," Chris broke in. "It was this harpsichordist from New York who told us how when you strike a harpsichord key the strings are plucked. They're not hit like on a piano."

Mr. Austin looked up with interest. He still wore his starched shirt and his tie was only slightly loosened. Brenda knew there was nothing he liked better than stimulating conversation at the dinner table, and Chris was doing her best to provide it.

"Wasn't that last piece she played great?" Chris suggested to Brenda. "The Mozart?"

Brenda looked at her stepsister's encouraging blue eyes and tried to understand what was happening. Chris knew that Brenda had been sent to the office that morning before the assembly; Brenda could tell from the expression on her face that Chris knew. But Brenda had the feeling her stepsister was covering for her and letting her know she had no intention of ratting.

"Yeah," Brenda concluded, "the Mozart piece at the end was the best."

Brenda's stepfather smiled warmly. With great relief Brenda piled another serving of broccoli onto her plate and continued to eat. Maybe it was going to be okay.

"How nice," Mrs. Austin commented from the other end of the table. "Bren, you didn't have assemblies like that at Arthur, did you?"

Brenda shrugged. It was a little hard trying to get enthusiastic about Kennedy considering all that had happened that day, even if Chris was keeping quiet about it. But Mrs. Austin was always trying to prove to Brenda how great it was that they had moved to Rose Hill — that it would be wonderful if Brenda just gave it a chance. It was the kind of comment that usually made Brenda feel like getting up from the table and bolting up to her room.

"Could I have the potatoes?" Chris asked suddenly.

Brenda lifted the dish and handed it to her stepsister. Chris seemed to pass her a significant glance. Mr. Austin didn't seem to notice.

Brenda's stepfather sat up straight in his chair and leaned forward. "Brenda, how's that essay coming for your English class? Will you have it ready by Monday?"

"It's all finished," Brenda answered quietly.

Brenda heard another fork clatter against its plate. Only this time it wasn't hers; it belonged to Chris. At the same time, Brenda felt three surprised faces looking up simultaneously from their dinner plates. She wanted to laugh. They were all shocked she had completed an assignment ahead of schedule. But they didn't know that the essay for Barnes's English class was something special.

"I just have to type it," Brenda added to make the event sound a little more normal. "I mean, it's not totally done."

"That's great!" Chris exclaimed. "I mean, Brenda that's . . . ah . . . ah . . . ah —"

Chris cut herself off with a huge sneeze that almost rattled the crystal. Mr. and Mrs. Austin administered blessings immediately. She gave a large, miserable sniff.

"Sorry," she apologized, brushing back a now loosened strand of blond hair. "I think I'm coming down with a bad cold."

"I thought your eyes looked glassy," Mrs. Austin said. "I want to take your temperature right after dinner. No going out if you're running a fever."

"I know."

Mr. Austin pushed his plate aside and tapped Brenda on the hand. "I'm very proud of you getting your paper done so early. Maybe you'll let us read it."

Brenda rolled her eyes.

"I'd like to see what you've written," he insisted.

"Jonathan," Mrs. Austin interrupted, "let Brenda make up her own mind."

Brenda was glad to see her mother give her stepfather a look that said "Don't push it." It was much too personal. She had written about Garfield House, the halfway house she had gone to the year before, when she ran away. The essay was also partly inspired by Tony Martinez, Brenda's favorite Garfield House counselor. Her stepfather couldn't accept Brenda's continued attachment to Garfield House, and the thought of sharing her essay with him made her get that familiar I-want-out-of-here feeling.

"If you feel like letting me see it when you get it back, I'd like to," Mr. Austin said quietly. "It's up to you." Brenda's mom smiled approvingly.

"Maybe," Brenda responded finally. "I'm finished eating. May I be excused?"

A series of looks passed from her mother to her stepfather and back again. Finally her mother nodded and Brenda took her plate into the kitchen.

Brenda leaned over the tile counter and rinsed her dish. She could hear the whispering in the dining room, Chris, her mom, and her stepfather discussing her again. For a moment she tried to listen, but she couldn't really hear their conversation. She stuck her plate in the dishwasher and hurried upstairs to her room.

Brenda was only half concentrating on her history book when she heard her stepsister pad across the hall outside her bedroom door. For a second the footsteps hesitated, and Brenda expected to hear a knock. Carefully Brenda turned down the classical music on her tiny tape player and lay very still. Then the footsteps changed direction until they faded away down the stairs.

Lying on her bed, her bare legs leaning against the wall, Brenda looked up at the ceiling. "This family is so weird," she said to herself. Then she slid down and let her head fall over the edge of the bed until her long, dark hair coasted on the shag carpet.

Sometimes those formal dinner table scenes made her want to stand up and make faces or dumb noises or pick up the bowl of perfectly

arranged carrots and dump them over her head —
anything to combat the Austin rigidity. But her
mom didn't seem to mind her husband's stiff personality, and neither did Chris. Maybe she was
the weird one.

At least Chris had not opened her mouth about
the trouble at school. That would have been all
Brenda needed. It was her cutting school last year
that led to the big blowout with her stepfather,
after he got that phone call from Mrs. Godwin.
And the big blowout led to her being grounded,
which led to her running away.

Just thinking about it made Brenda's stomach
feel tight, and she hugged herself to ease the tension. Still, as Tony Martinez told her so often, that
was in the past. She didn't have to hang on to that
garbage anymore. With an awkward back somer-
sault, Brenda rolled off her bed and walked over
to her desk to look at her essay for Mr. Barnes.

The paper about Garfield House was held down
by her earring jar and a pine cone Tony had given
her. Brenda moved the jar and carefully placed
the pine cone on the shelf above the desk. She read
the essay over.

The pages were filled with erasures, cross outs,
misspelled words, and words connected only by
arrows, but Brenda took a proud breath as she
looked it over. The assignment had been to write
an essay about someone who had taken a different
path in life. The class had read *The Road Not
Taken*, the poem by Robert Frost that told about
a traveler who took a side road and found that it
changed his life.

The poem had excited Brenda. It made her think of Tony Martinez and all the kids at the halfway house. All of them were different, either because of the problems they faced at home or because they were unable to deal with school or their families. And Tony made a real difference to all those kids. Lately he had asked Brenda to counsel younger kids — that was making a difference in the way she felt about herself. When Barnes assigned the essay, Brenda knew she had to write about Tony and the house. She had never before allowed a school assignment to be so personal, so much a part of her.

"Just read that essay, Chris," Brenda said to herself. "Just look at that and tell me I'm not as good as you and your friends."

Feeling calm and loose, Brenda turned her Mozart tape back up and did a slow dance to it. She caught a glimpse of herself in the mirror. Her slender limbs were stretching this way and that in her cut-off shorts, heavy cotton socks, and black sweat shirt. Slowing her movements, Brenda moved to the mirror and made a face. Her features were angular: narrow nose, wide mouth, sharp cheekbones. She wondered if her large eyes exposed every bit of confusion she felt. Brenda tried to find a new, mysterious expression. She was trying an over-the-shoulder glare when she heard a loud knock on her door.

Instinctively Brenda clicked off the tape machine. She stepped in front of her desk so that whoever was at the door couldn't see her essay.

"Who is it?"

"Me, Chris."

Brenda turned over all the pages, prepared herself with a deep breath, and opened the door. Chris was now wearing a terry cloth robe over her white sweat suit. One of the robe pockets was overflowing with tissues, and Chris's nose was red. Even though she looked less composed than usual, Chris still had that air of blond perfection that always made Brenda feel so unrefined and awkward.

"What is it?" Brenda asked cautiously, guarding the entrance to her room.

"I just wanted to tell you that my cold has now been officially diagnosed by Catherine as the flu." Chris sniffed.

"Oh." Brenda paused. She didn't know why Chris was making an announcement. "Do you feel bad?"

"Just stuffed up and kind of weak. It's getting worse." Chris smiled blearily and continued to stand at the door.

"Well, I hope you feel better."

"I'm staying home tonight," Chris rambled. "You know Dad's policy. No going out if you have a fever. Maybe Ted will come over and watch TV." Chris cleared her throat nervously and flicked her long blonde hair behind her shoulder. "Can I come in? I don't think I'm too contagious."

Brenda hesitated. "I guess."

Chris entered Brenda's room and carefully closed the door behind her. She gave her stepsister a tentative smile before being caught off guard by a violent sneeze.

"Gesundheit, or whatever," Brenda mumbled as she sat in her desk chair.

"So, how are you?" Chris asked with a forced cheerfulness. She blew her nose. Brenda suspected there was something very specific on Chris's mind. Brenda recalled Chris's silence at the dinner table over the trouble at school. She prepared herself to find out what Chris expected in exchange.

"I'm okay," she began cautiously. "I mean, I'm not sick." There was an awkward pause. "Um, thanks for not telling about. . . ." Brenda waited and checked the look in Chris's eyes.

"That's okay," Chris answered in a whisper. "I figured you didn't really deserve to get sent to the office. I'd never tell Dad."

The conversation halted again, and Chris peered around Brenda to the papers on her desk. Brenda guarded her essay with an arm.

"So you really finished your assignment for Barnes?"

Brenda nodded.

Chris's blue eyes brightened and her face broke into a wide smile. "This is so perfect!" She pulled a folded sheet of paper out of her other bathrobe pocket and put the paper on Brenda's bed. It was a form with Chris's name written at the top.

"Oh, this is going to work out great," Chris smiled again at Brenda. "You know the school ski trip I signed up for? The one to Mount Jackson?"

Brenda shook her head vaguely. She intentionally tried to stay unaware of the details of her sister's social life.

Chris continued. "It's tomorrow, just for the

day. Ted and I are signed up for it. Anyway, Dad said I absolutely cannot go tomorrow since I have a temperature, and I didn't want to waste my ticket — I mean it's all paid for and the snow is supposed to be getting really good, so. . . ." Chris paused to blow her nose.

Brenda had the feeling her sister was avoiding arriving at the point. "So?"

"So, I asked Catherine if it was okay if I gave my place to you and she said it was. So here." Chris held out the reservation form. "You get to go!"

There was a long silence. Brenda tried to fight the tightening in her jaw. Chris was doing it again — she was trying to push Brenda into the Kennedy social scene, a place she didn't belong and didn't want to.

"What makes you think I want to go skiing with a bunch of people from school?" Brenda heard the hostile edge in her voice, but she didn't care if Chris heard it or not.

"Brenda, it's not like you won't know anybody. I talked to Phoebe and she said she just decided to go herself. She said she'd love it if you came. She offered to give you a ride."

Brenda continued to stare angrily at her sister. Chris really had it all planned. Sure, Phoebe was usually nice to Brenda, but Phoebe wouldn't be the only one there. Besides, Brenda didn't even know Phoebe well enough to have a five minute conversation with her.

"Isn't Sasha Jenkins in Barnes's English class with you?" Chris asked cheerily.

25

"Yeah, so?"

"Sasha's going, too. You can all ski together. Phoebe and Sasha both want you to go." Chris paused to cough and sniff. "Come on, what better have you got to do?"

"I was going to go to Garfield House. There's a new kid Tony wants me to talk to." Brenda almost never missed a Saturday at Garfield House. Of course, Chris would never accept a visit to the halfway house as a worthwhile reason to give up anything.

"Brenda, I think it would be good if you tried to make some new friends at school. It's not good for you to just hang out with those kids at Garfield. You should try to make some other friends, too. I think you'd be a lot happier if you did."

"I don't have any ski clothes."

"You know you can borrow mine. Most people are renting boots and skis up on the mountain. If there's anything you need, I'll loan it to you."

Brenda looked at the desk behind her. "I still have to type my essay for Barnes. You know how bad my handwriting is."

"You can do it on Sunday."

"I'm not a very good skier."

"Then go and practice and you'll get better." Chris stood up and stuck her hands in her pockets. "You can give me as many excuses as you want. Why don't you just admit that you're scared to go?"

Brenda looked up sharply. She felt her adrenaline start to pump. "I'm not scared."

Chris stared at her. "Then why won't you go?

You haven't given me one good reason. The only thing I can figure out is that you're afraid of my friends, afraid they won't like you or something."

"I'm not afraid of your friends," Brenda scoffed with a slight laugh.

"Well then, why won't you go? You act like I'm asking you to face a firing squad or something."

"I do not."

"Why don't you trust me for once? I didn't tell on you about getting caught for cutting, did I?"

Brenda stopped. So that was it, Chris was calling in her favor. She hadn't said anything about Brenda's trip to the office, so now Brenda had to go skiing.

Chris smiled reassuringly. "Brenda, it'll be fun. My friends aren't so bad. You'll see. If you're worried about being alone, they'll take care of you. Honest."

"Sure they will." Brenda's voice dripped sarcasm.

"The real truth is you're just afraid. You like to act tough and everything, but the truth is that —"

"I'm not afraid," Brenda said grimly.

"Then take my place and go up to Mount Jackson tomorrow," Chris challenged. "It's only for one day. If you're really not scared, then you'll go."

"Okay," Brenda spat. "I'll go!"

Suddenly the room was quiet. Chris had a peaceful smile on her face. "Good," she said in a self-satisfied voice. She placed her reservation form on top of Brenda's essay and started to leave the room. Chris stopped in the doorway and coughed. "Phoebe will pick you up tomorrow at seven. I'll bring you a stack of all my ski stuff and you can take what you want."

"Thanks a lot," Brenda muttered coldly.

"Don't be so sure you are going to have such an awful time. You might be surprised."

"Sure."

Chris smiled. "Don't worry. My friends will take care of you."

A second later the bedroom door swung shut and Chris was gone.

Chapter
3

It was a perfect day for skiing — brisk and clear, without a trace of wind or moisture. The sun was just coming up and the grass was topped with a paper-thin sheet of ice. As Sasha Jenkins marched across the Kennedy athletic field toward the parking lot, the frozen layer crunched under her steps.

Sasha thought about the ice — water changing into ice and back into water, sort of like the Eastern philosophy her father talked about all the time. Biting her lip, she wondered if she could turn that thought into an essay for Mr. Barnes's English class. The composition was due Monday, and she hadn't even begun writing yet. She really shouldn't have been going skiing at all, but since most of the crowd had signed up, she couldn't stay home.

"Something that makes a difference," she whispered, reminding herself of the assigned theme for Barnes's essay.

If she could just figure out what to write about, she'd be home free. Maybe she'd have to stay up all night to wait until she was really tired and her creativity could flow. Sometimes she worked that way when she had assignments for the newspaper. Flinging back her dark, heavy hair, Sasha took a deep, meditative breath.

She was the first one in the parking lot. She had declined when Peter offered her a ride, because she hoped watching the dawn might give her inspiration for her essay.

Taking out two large barrettes, Sasha sat on the retaining wall next to the flagpole and clipped back the sides of her hair. She was just stretching her arms over her hair when the first car pulled in. A tall, thin girl emerged from the blue sedan. Sasha was surprised that Janie Barstow was coming on the ski trip. Janie was painfully shy and didn't usually participate in school social events. Sasha knew her as Peter Lacey's assistant at WKND, the Kennedy High radio station.

"Hi, Janie," Sasha said. Trying to make Janie feel comfortable, Sasha slid over and offered her a seat. "I didn't know you were a skier."

"I'm not," Janie said in a wispy voice. "I've never been before. I'm taking those beginning lessons." She didn't sound enthusiastic.

"So am I!" Sasha said brightly. "I've only skied twice myself, and that was cross-country, so I figured I'd better take lessons, too. Maybe we can ski together!"

Janie kicked her feet and looked down. She stuck her hands in the pockets of her oversized parka. "If you really want to."

"It'll be fun. I promise not to laugh at you if you promise not to laugh at me."

Janie smiled tentatively. "Okay. But I'm really only going because my mom thought it sounded like fun. I'm not very good at stuff like this."

Sasha gave Janie a sympathetic look. She had talked to Mrs. Barstow at her parents' bookstore. Janie's mother had even asked Sasha's advice about good school clubs. No wonder Janie was not excited about the ski trip.

Sasha tried to cheer her up. "Who *is* good at this stuff?" she said sweetly. "Chris Austin is the only ski ace I know, and she's not coming. Phoebe's even lamer than I am. Woody's all style, but not much else. Ted barely knows what he's doing, but he's so nervy he'll try anything." Janie laughed softly and Sasha continued. "Peter's probably the same as Ted —"

Sasha stopped midsentence. It was impossible not to notice the sudden look of panic on Janie's face. Her big brown eyes grew huge and her mouth fell slightly open.

"Janie, what is it?"

Janie let her head fall forward. "It's just weird to see Peter." She halted. "You know, since I quit the radio station. Every time I run into him he keeps asking me to come back."

"Oh, right." Now it was Sasha who felt self-conscious. She should have been more sensitive about mentioning Peter Lacey. She had forgotten

31

Janie had quit the station. It had been obvious Janie had a terrible crush on Peter, and that Peter only thought of her as a friend.

Janie brushed the hair out of her eyes and moved close to Sasha. "Laurie Bennington's not coming today, is she?"

"I'm sure she's not. Don't worry. She wouldn't dare go anywhere around any of us now." Sasha looked straight ahead. It even hurt her to remember how Laurie had humiliated Janie. Laurie had intentionally led the shy girl to think that Peter wanted to take her to the Homecoming Dance, in order to embarrass Peter for having snubbed Laurie. Thinking about it still made Sasha angry. At least Laurie had been properly rewarded when her plan backfired and was now keeping a very low profile at school. "I wouldn't worry about Laurie anymore if I were you," Sasha comforted.

"Do you really think so?"

"Honest. Don't worry."

Janie sighed and lightly kicked the wall.

The two girls sat in silence and watched the cars that were beginning to pull into the parking lot. The bus still hadn't appeared, so when Peter's beige Volkswagen zipped up to them, Janie had no excuse to flee. She hovered next to Sasha and looked toward the main office building.

The bug chugged to a stop in front of them, and as soon as the motor clunked off, the passenger door flung open. Ted bolted out and rushed to unlatch the pair of skis tied to the back bumper.

"Hi, Sasha," he called. Ted pulled on his letterman's jacket and rubbed his hands together as he examined the ski rack.

Next, Woody pushed his way out of the back seat. He was wearing a thick sweater, suspenders, and blue jeans. His bushy hair was trying to escape from under his knit stocking cap. Reaching back, he pulled out a pair of beat-up plastic ski boots.

"Sash, I brought my sister's old ski boots for you. See if they fit on your big feet." He handed her the boots.

"Wow. Thanks." Sasha slipped off a clog and shoved her foot into a boot. "They fit!"

Woody leaned over and grinned at Janie. "Hi, Janie!"

Janie's greeting was barely audible.

"Webster," called Ted, "come back here and help get these skis down. The latch is stuck."

Woody rolled his eyes and scurried to the back of the car. Janie was still looking in the other direction when Peter finally appeared on the driver's side. But Sasha could see the tension in Janie's slender body as Peter stood and pulled a fisherman's-knit sweater over his head. When his rugged face popped through the neck, he spotted his former assistant.

"Janie! Hey, how are you?" His voice was warm, but Sasha could tell that he was a little uncomfortable, too.

Janie didn't look at him. "Fine."

Peter came closer. Sasha sensed that Janie didn't want to be left alone and stayed near her.

"Hi, Peter," Sasha said cheerily. "Aren't these boots great?" She held out a heavy booted foot. Janie stared at it as if the boot was the most interesting thing in the world.

"Have you heard anything from Lisa?" Sasha

asked. Peter's girl friend, Lisa Chang, had moved to Colorado to train full-time as a figure skater.

Peter brightened as soon as he heard Lisa's name. "I called her last night. She's kind of lonely, but she's really high on her new coach. She said to tell everybody hello. Especially you, Janie."

Janie had to look up. As soon as she met Peter's eye her cheeks began to redden. "Tell her hello from me, too."

"Sure."

"How's the station?" Janie managed.

"Not too cool. I just got a new assistant, but he's a real dufus. Some freshman named Kevin."

Sasha noticed a tiny smile on Janie's face.

"It's a joke," Peter went on. "Sometimes I have to play these doggo records just because I can't find the decent ones."

Peter looked back over to his car. Woody and Ted were still trying to get the skis down. "Are you sure you don't want to come back to the station?" he asked suddenly.

Janie blushed even redder. "Peter, I —"

"How about if I made you station manager, you know, with a title and all? Every time I went on the air I'd say your name. How about that?"

"I don't think so," Janie said weakly.

Sasha couldn't stand watching Janie be so uncomfortable. Janie could never go back to the station, and Sasha knew it. If Peter hadn't thought that WKND was the most important thing in the world, he would have known it, too.

"The station needs you," Peter pleaded.

"Well. . . ." Janie hesitated, starting to buckle under the strength of Peter's personality.

It was impossible for Sasha not to interrupt. "But, Janie, I thought you wanted to volunteer for the newspaper," she improvised. "You won't have time to do both, will you?"

Janie looked at Sasha as though she had just saved Janie's life. "That's right," she told Peter. "I'm going to work on the newspaper. I decided that's what I want to do now."

"Oh. I didn't know that." Peter shrugged in humble defeat. "Well, I tried," he said. "I'm sure you'll be great on the newspaper, too." With a tight smile, Peter walked back to join Woody and Ted.

"Thanks," Janie whispered to Sasha. The two girls walked to the edge of the athletic field. "I just didn't know what to say."

"That's okay. You don't have to work on the paper, you know." Sasha looked up in anticipation. "Unless you want to, that is. I mean, we could really use you."

Janie looked back toward the guys and pulled on her bangs. "Maybe I will," she said finally. "It would make my mother happy."

Sasha grinned and patted Janie on the arm. "It will make me and the rest of the newspaper staff happy, too."

"Hey everybody," Woody suddenly yelled. "I see a big yellow school bus pulling into the parking lot."

Sasha gestured for Janie to come with her, and they headed toward the bus.

"Maybe I should have let it warm up longer," Phoebe said in exasperation as she tapped on the steering wheel of her mother's station wagon. She and Brenda were only halfway to Kennedy and the car had just stalled for the fourth time. "I hope we don't miss the bus."

Brenda bit her tongue. Missing the bus sounded like the perfect solution to the hopeless situation that lay ahead of her. She had been up since four-thirty, worrying, pacing, praying, trying to figure out a way to escape this day of torture called a ski trip. Maybe her prayers were being answered. No, the engine had quit coughing, and the car was moving ahead. Brenda slumped in her seat.

"Did you bring another pair of pants?" Phoebe asked in a self-consciously friendly tone.

Brenda looked at her tight striped jeans. She had decided to decline Chris's offer of ski clothes and had worn her own concoction instead — jeans, turtleneck, big black sweater, and a yellow cotton bandana. It didn't seem to make any sense now, but she wasn't about to admit that in front of Phoebe.

"Not really, but these are stretchy," Brenda said. She clutched her beret and gloves in her tight, tense hands.

Phoebe smiled and flicked on the radio. She was wearing wool knickers and a green sweater that showed off her red hair. "I just meant those will get wet pretty fast. Especially if you're as big a klutz as I am." Phoebe gave a short, self-deprecating laugh.

"I'll be okay."

"I brought two extra pairs of pants and some long underwear. You're welcome to borrow."

"Thanks."

"Sure."

Brenda tried to calm herself. It was just a ski trip and Phoebe was trying to be nice. It would be over in a few hours. When it was, Brenda would have proved something to both herself and her sister. She just had to ride it out.

Phoebe sang a few bars with the radio. Her voice was clear and pleasant. "Are you a good skier?" she finally asked.

Brenda shrugged. The last time she had gone skiing she had just learned to parallel. She hoped she still remembered how.

"I bet you're like Chris," Phoebe volunteered. "She's such a good athlete. I had to sign up for lessons myself."

Brenda didn't say anything. Of course Chris was as disgustingly good at skiing as she was at everything else. It was just another comparison where Brenda came up short.

"We did this same trip last year, and a bunch of kids raced down the green run. Chris beat them all. It was amazing. When she got to the bottom, all she could do was tell me how she should have taken another five seconds off her time." Phoebe glanced at Brenda and laughed. "But that's Chris."

Brenda laughed as well. She couldn't help it. Phoebe really knew Chris, warts and all. That realization made Brenda feel safer and warmer toward Phoebe. She didn't want to see people put Chris down, but it was good to hear a person who really knew Chris admit that she wasn't totally perfect.

"Here we are," Phoebe announced. She turned left into the Kennedy parking lot. She turned off

37

the ignition then stared into the rearview mirror.

Brenda turned to see a silver Honda zip by and pull into the other end of the lot. Immediately Phoebe reached over and restarted the engine. She followed the Honda and managed to pull into the space beside it. She smiled at Brenda a second time and turned off the engine. It was a quick, slightly conspiratorial smile.

Phoebe did not open her car door right away. She was looking at herself in a mirrored blush case, adjusting the color of her cheeks. Brenda saw a boy get out of the Honda and walk back to untie his skis from the rack on the roof. He was tall and broad-shouldered and wore a professional-looking jumpsuit. A red sweater was slung over his shoulders. He quickly unlatched his skis as if he'd taken them down a thousand times.

Finally he turned to reach for something in the front seat and Brenda recognized him. Even she knew Brad Davidson. Brad's face was handsome and regular, but with a chipped tooth that kept him from looking like those stereotyped handsome guys on billboards. Now she understood why Phoebe had parked on this side of the lot. Until recently, Phoebe had been Brad's girl friend.

"Might as well get out."

Brenda started to go but halted when she saw the busload of people waiting across the lot, most of whom she didn't even recognize. Suddenly, the whole thing was very real. Too real. Brenda looked back for Phoebe. Compared to the kids inside the bus, Phoebe was an old friend.

But Phoebe was hanging back by the silver Honda, waiting for Brad to finish gathering his things. When he started for the bus, Phoebe put her hand on his arm to stop him. Brenda stood close by and waited.

"Hi," Phoebe said, her voice soft and apologetic.

Brad looked up edgily. "I didn't know you were going to be here." He didn't sound happy about it.

"I just decided yesterday."

"I wish I'd known," Brad answered.

Feeling as if she was eavesdropping on something private, Branda walked a few yards away. The couple didn't seem to notice her. In fact, Brad seemed to be deliberately trying not to notice anything. He closed his car door firmly and gathered his equipment. As he started to walk toward the bus, Phoebe stopped him.

"Brad, let's sit together on the bus."

"How come?"

"I'd like to talk," Phoebe said firmly. "Find out what's going on with you.

"No thanks."

"Are you going to stay mad at me forever?"

Brad's face was now hard and unforgiving. There was a terrible sadness in his brown eyes. His only answer was to flinch and walk away.

Phoebe watched him go, her pretty face clouded with disappointment. Brenda could see Phoebe was hurt by Brad's reaction. She walked over and tapped her sister's best friend on the arm.

"Phoebe, are you okay?"

Phoebe tried to avoid Brenda's eyes, then stepped away.

"I don't want to talk about it."

"Okay, I didn't mean to —"

Phoebe raised one hand and abruptly turned

39

her face away. Then she began to walk stiffly toward the bus, following the path of her ex-boyfriend.

Brenda stopped. What a way to begin this trip, she thought. The one person she was beginning to think of as a friend had just deserted her. Brenda suddenly had that old urge to run — run so fast and so far that no one would find her. She was just looking for the best route out when she heard someone call her.

"Brenda!"

Brenda looked back over at the bus.

"Hey, Brenda, what are you just standing there for? C'mon, we've saved you a seat."

Brenda saw Ted waving out the bus window. Phoebe was in the bus now, and Sasha was also waving. If she turned and walked off now, everybody would see her.

Brenda took one last look at the street, tapped the hood of Phoebe's car, and began walking quickly toward the bus.

Chapter
4

The bus was almost ready to go. Sasha sat with Phoebe, Brenda, Peter, and Ted near the front. Janie was just behind the driver, and Brad was in the back. Woody seemed to be somewhere in between, although he periodically jumped up from one group and ran to begin a conversation with another. As usual, there was not enough of Woody to go around. Even the bus driver seemed to notice.

"Hey, you in the curly hair."

Woody looked up from the seat behind Sasha where he was draped, his arms looped in a big O. "Which do you mean?" Woody answered, winking at Sasha. "The pretty one in the long, curly hair or the funny-looking one in the short, curly hair?"

Everybody laughed and for a second even the bus driver smiled. Then his voice got gruff again, "You, the funny-looking one. Quit jumping around if you expect me to get this thing going up the mountain."

"That's right," Miss Offenbacher chimed from the front. She was a science teacher at Kennedy and had volunteered for the hazardous duty of ski club advisor.

"Okay, okay," Woody conceded as he suddenly sat up straight and folded his arms. "I promise not to move until we get to the mountain."

"Well, in that case I guess we can get going," Miss Offenbacher replied. "Mr. Lutz. . . ."

The driver nodded and turned the key as a cheer went up in the bus. He released the brake, put the bus in gear, and the Kennedy ski expedition was almost on its way when a squeal of brakes and a roar of an engine made every single head on the bus turn.

"Uh oh," Ted cautioned. "Mr. Macho himself."

There was a general groan as a horn blared out from the yellow old Trans Am that was speeding next to the bus. Suddenly it pulled ahead and cut over.

"John Marquette," Peter said, pulling the headphones of his tape player away from his ears. "You'd at least think he could be on time."

"Why does he want to ride with us anyway?" Sasha asked. "He's got that totally repulsive car."

"That's it," Woody explained. "Any girl who saw him drive up in that thing would be so grossed out that she wouldn't ski with him. Hey, Ted, guess what Marquette's idea of a fun evening is?"

"What?"

"Racing a trash compactor to see who can squash the most empty beer cans."

"Yeah, but a trash compactor has more personality."

Nobody laughed this time. The bus driver had stopped on Miss Offenbacher's orders.

Ted groaned, "Mr. Macho is joining us."

Everyone turned to look as Marquette's brakes squealed again and he exploded from the driver's seat. Grabbing an armful of ski gear, he slammed the car door and strutted toward the bus. Sasha shuddered to look at him. Tall and beefy, he was wearing tight beige cords, a short black parka, and a pair of mirrored sunglasses. His dark hair was cropped short and his face was large and heavy featured.

"Ever since he won that all city wrestling title he's been out of control," Peter said.

"I know," Ted replied. "He started about five fights during football. The first couple of times I didn't think it was his fault, but then I figured it out. He's a real jerk."

The boys grew quiet as Marquette stood next to the bus driver and surveyed the busload, hands on hips. When he spotted the crowd, his full mouth curled up on one side.

The bus was moving again, but Marquette hesitated before taking a seat. He slid his sunglasses to the top of his head and smiled hungrily. "Hey, Sasha," he crooned, leaning his bulky body over the armrest. "Hey, foxette, didn't I see you at my meet last week? Pretty impressive, huh?"

Sasha rolled her eyes and faced forward. "I was only there because I had to cover it for the newspaper, John," she said bluntly.

43

"Sure, sure." He laughed. "Maybe I'll see you on the slopes, little fox."

"John, sit down!" Miss Offenbacher ordered.

"Don't rush me, I'm going," Marquette growled. He reached forward and tousled Sasha's hair before lumbering back and spreading himself and his gear over two seats.

In less than an hour, the bus reached the mountains and started to climb. Ted had slipped over to a seat next to Brad. Brad was sitting in the very last row. He had his ski boots stacked on the seat next to him as if to protect himself from anyone who wanted to get too close — mainly Phoebe, Ted thought. As Ted slid in, Brad moved the boots to let his friend sit down.

Brad looked toward the bus entrance, but at that moment Phoebe turned back. Immediately he folded his arms over his chest and slid down in his seat. "I wouldn't have come if I'd known she was going to be here," he grumbled.

Ted rolled his eyes. He took off his letterman's jacket and pushed up the sleeves of his sweater. "Come off it, Davidson. How long has it been since you guys broke up? Two months? Don't you think it's time to move on?"

Brad shrugged moodily.

"I know this other girl who goes to Breakstone Private. She's great. I went out with her last year — don't tell Chris." Ted grinned and nudged Brad with his elbow. "Want to go out with her?"

"Uh uh."

"C'mon, you'll love her. She's really a good person and —"

"Forget it."

44

Ted looked at the floor and sighed. "I guess I'm not being too subtle, am I?"

This time Brad managed to laugh. "No, I guess not. I know why you're trying to do it, and I appreciate it. If I were you and you were me I'd probably be doing the same thing."

"It's okay. I understand. Sort of."

"Where is Chris?" Brad asked.

"She's got the flu. Her father made her stay home. It was probably a good idea, I don't think she feels too good. Brenda came instead. She's up front with the gang, but she doesn't look like she's having a very good time."

"I saw her when I ran into Phoebe by the car. I thought she never came on stuff like this."

"She usually doesn't."

"So you're on your own?" Brad gave him a teasing smile. "Better watch it, wildman."

Ted waved him off. "Nah. Chris promised no sympathy if I break my leg doing stunts on the green run." Ted paused and grinned. "So what's the point?"

Brad laughed.

Ted moved in and continued in a sly voice. "We could try one race down that one side of the run, the really hairy slope you beat me on last year. I bet Peter would go in on it, too."

Brad turned back to the window. "No thanks. I think I'm going to go off on my own today."

"Come on, Brad. . . ."

"I know. It's just that when I feel like this I just want to be alone."

Ted looked down at his hands. "All right. If that's what you really want to do."

45

"It is."

"Okay." Ted got up and gave his friend a light slap on the back.

"Thanks anyway," Brad said. "See you later." He turned back and stared moodily out at the snow.

Ted shook his head and made his way back up the aisle to rejoin the crowd.

Chapter
5

"'My friends will take care of you,'" Brenda mumbled to herself. "Sure, Chris. Sure." Brenda trudged out of the rental hut carrying her skis and poles.

She stared at the endless white before her. The sun was bright, the surrounding trees tall and picturesque. The cold made her skin tingle and the air was perfectly clean. Two kids in snowsuits were tossing snowballs at each other and squealing with delight. Each happy shout made Brenda feel even lonelier. Her worst fears had come true.

The crowd was back inside the rental chalet, probably still laughing at Woody and having a great time. Even Phoebe, who was in a bad mood all morning, was in on the fun. But not Brenda. She had started this trip an outsider and she would continue to be one after the whole crummy day was over. It wouldn't have been so bad if she could have stuck with Sasha. But Sasha and

Phoebe had signed up for lessons, and expert skier Chris had not. Brenda couldn't exactly race down the hardest slopes with Ted and Peter Lacey.

Brenda let one ski plop down to the ground, held onto the other, and tried to stick her two poles in the snow with one hand. The thickly padded gloves made it awkward, and she had to poke the poles into the snow several times before they stood up straight. The surface was icy and the ski on the ground started to slide back toward the rental hut. Brenda stopped it with her boot and let out a cloudy huff. Great. All she needed now was to make a total fool of herself on the slope.

"Darn it," Brenda muttered as she repositioned the ski and secured the leather strap around her ankle. She didn't want to set the world on fire. She would have been perfectly content if she had one or two decent runs on an easy hill, just to feel the sun on her cheeks and the cold air through her hair. If she could get these skis adjusted, she could find her way to a run that she could handle. Chris probably wouldn't like it — Brenda skiing by herself really defeated the whole unstated purpose behind the trip — but Chris was just going to have to learn she couldn't plan other people's lives for them.

Brenda leaned all the way over as she stepped into her first binding. She put her heel down, then her toe, twisting the lock at the front. Nothing happened.

"Darn."

She tried again. More pressure on the metal plate didn't seem to help. Throwing her hair back and biting off one of her gloves, Brenda now put the bare heel of her hand against the cold metal while trying to wedge the binding with her foot. Still nothing.

"This is ridiculous."

Brenda decided to try the other ski. She popped right in, but the bad binding still wouldn't work. In desperation, she tried to stand on one leg and grab at the loose ski, but the surface was slick underneath, and she found her feet shooting forward. She worked to regain her balance by waving her arms, but it was no use. She was going to fall.

"Watch it!" a voice warned.

Brenda felt a pair of strong male arms catch her around the waist.

"These dumb skis." Brenda clutched wildly at the hands around her until she managed to regain her balance.

"They never take care of that rental stuff," the voice responded. The arms held her until Brenda was steady, then released her. Brenda turned to see her rescuer. It was Brad Davidson.

"What's the problem?" Brad asked coolly. He had stepped back and was staring at the entrance to the rental hut.

"I can't get the binding to lock. Maybe it's broken," Brenda told him nervously.

For a second he didn't respond, he was still watching the door to the chalet. Then he knelt down next to her and started to examine the troublesome binding.

"Let me have a look," he said in a preoccupied voice. Taking off his blue and yellow ski gloves, he twisted a small bolt with his fingers. "Try it again," he suggested. Brenda put her foot on the ski and Brad easily snapped the toe piece in place.

"There you go."

"Thanks."

Brad nodded and looked back toward the hut. He put his sunglasses on and pulled his skis from a nearby mound of snow. Ignoring Brenda, he wiped the flakes off the highly waxed surface.

Brenda pulled her gloves back on and tried to remember how to move on skis. A few swift pushes with her poles brought it back to her. She looked in the direction of the chair lifts, pulled her beret out of her back pocket, and adjusted it over her ears. After skiing a few yards she stopped. She had no idea which lift to take.

For a few minutes, she stood there and stared at the mountains. It was hard to tell which lift was which. Brenda looked around to find another skier who seemed about her speed. If she found someone who skied like she did, she could just follow that person to the right slope. But before she could spot another novice she heard the light shushing of skis. Brad was next to her, gliding easily in front of her in a flashy racing stop.

"Hi. He smiled. His distant air was gone.

"Hi."

"You're Brenda Austin, right? I've seen you tons of times with Chris, but we've never really met."

Brenda tried to smile.

"Ted told me about Chris getting the flu."

"Yeah."

"Too bad." Brad pulled his gloves on and looked around. "You going on the blue run first?"

Brenda didn't answer. She didn't know what to say.

Brad's brown eyes opened wider. "You taking the green?"

"Sure," Brenda said quickly.

"I'll go with you. Come on." He put his hand on the small of her back and gave a gentle nudge.

Brenda began to ski. Brad stayed right by her side until Brenda felt him hesitate and look back toward the chalet once again.

Brenda caught a glimpse of a small figure standing in front of the rental hut. Even from across the meadow, she knew it was Phoebe. She was standing, skis and poles in hand, staring at Brad and Brenda. Brenda felt her body lurch to one side. She had to concentrate on her skiing. She made herself forget about Phoebe, and focused all her energy on her body. She had to survive this day on the slopes without looking like a real fool.

Brad skied on.

"Did you bring sunglasses?" Brad asked Brenda. His tone was cool and distant. They had been standing in the lift line for at least five minutes; this was the first time he'd spoken.

"No."

Brenda wished she had. Dark glasses would have hidden her discomfort. As they waited in the long line for the chair lift, Brenda wondered what she'd gotten herself into.

After his initial warmth, Brad ignored her. He was even cooler and more preoccupied than he'd been when he fixed her binding. Why did Brad want to ski with her in the first place? Had Chris talked to him, too? Brad, please be nice to my poor sister Brenda. Ask her to ski with you. Just make the effort and then you can ignore her — like Phoebe and the rest of them.

"Better be careful," Brad said. "The sun is really strong today."

Brad had sharp tan lines around his eyes. This ski trip was obviously not his first trip of the season. His brown hair was streaked with blond, his nose slightly sunburned.

The attendant was holding the lift chair so that Brenda and Brad could sit. Brenda landed with a plop and the lift carried them up. The ground was silently and quickly rushing away, the wind was growing colder and the air thinner. Brenda looked at Brad. He was staring down at his skis.

"Have you skied Jackson before?"

Brad looked off toward another slope. "Yeah, a lot."

They climbed higher.

"You like it?"

"Mmmmm."

Brenda gave up, and they continued in silence. As the chair was lifted higher and higher, the gray concrete rental hut and wooden chalet faded further into the distance.

Suddenly Brenda noticed the sharp grade of the hill beneath them. She began to worry that they were headed up a very difficult slope and she would not be able to make it down. Brad was staring out across the horizon and seemed perfectly content to endure the rest of the ride wordlessly. Brenda fidgeted with her beret and decided she wasn't going to ask him for any help once they got to the top. No way.

The lift swung gracefully onto the platform and Brenda readied herself to ski off the chair and down the ramp. Unfortunately, she found herself so anxious that when her skis finally touched down her legs felt wobbly. In a second, Brad had her and kept hold of her arm as they skied onto the snow. Awkwardly, Brenda disengaged herself from Brad and straightened her black sweater.

"Have you been up here before?" Brad questioned.

Brenda looked down at her boots and nervously tapped her pole into the snow. "Sure. It's just my first time this year."

Brad was staring at her. "Which run do you want to take?" There was a wooden map behind him with color-coded arrows to all the trails.

"The green," Brenda blurted out, not really knowing a thing about any of them. She hoped the green was comparatively easy.

"Don't you want to warm up first?"

"I'll warm up on the way down."

"Boy, if you warm up on the green run, you're going to blow me away. I never ski that run first time out."

Brenda felt her insides tightening. It sounded like the green run was going to be instant suicide. At least Brad had said he didn't like to ski it first thing.

"Then why don't you go down the other run by yourself?" she suggested casually. If Brenda could encourage Brad to go off on his own, then she could inch down the mountain by herself.

"Are you sure you want to go down that run?"

"Yeah. You go on by yourself." Brenda tried to sound nonchalant. "Look, it's better not to cramp each other's style, right? Maybe I'll see you at the bottom."

Brad didn't budge. He looked a little worried.

"Go ahead," Brenda said again. "Go on."

He continued to stare at her as if he was calling her bluff. There was no backing out. She would just have to take off and get out of sight as soon as she could — then she could stretch out into a clumsy snowplow or just sit down, take an easy fall, and stop. She sidestepped to the top of the green run.

"See you later," Brenda called with as much enthusiasm as she could muster. She pushed off hard with her poles and felt the wind burn her eyes as she started to descend.

She managed to make a fairly decent showing as she rounded the first curve. Amazingly, her skis were still parallel. A few more yards and she would be out of Brad's view. But before she knew it, Brenda was picking up speed and the turns were getting narrower. She had no choice but to take them or risk plowing right into a tree.

She managed to lean left and a huge spray of powdered snow shot out from under her, but Brenda had no sooner made that curve than she saw another one coming at her, and the slope was getting steeper and steeper! She brought her skis even closer together and this time shifted her weight in the opposite direction. Her turn was way too wide — she skirted the edge of the forest —

54

but Brenda somehow managed to miss smashing into the trees.

Brenda's heart was pounding and her legs were almost shaking, she was trying so hard to control them. She hit another bump and her skis jumped three or four inches off the ground. She came back down with a jolt, lost her balance, her arms flailing wildly, and her skis beginning to shoot out from under her. She was headed straight for the tree line.

"Brenda!" She suddenly heard a shout from behind her. "Watch out!"

Brenda saw the tree coming at her and careened out of control, tumbling sideways, her shoulder first hitting the snow with a hard bounce. She felt her body flipping and took a mouth and face full of snow, but still she kept going. She had somehow missed the trees, but her skis wouldn't come off. Please, please, Brenda thought, let me come out of these skis. Finally one of her bindings snapped and then the other. She continued to tumble, and the unwieldy skis, attached by the safety binders to her ankles, fell hard against her legs in the downward scramble. Brenda got another face full of snow, another hard bump, and then she stopped, face down, spread out like a Raggedy Ann doll.

"Brenda!"

Brenda recognized the voice now but didn't look up. She didn't want to. It was too humiliating, and Brad was the last person she wanted to see.

"Brenda, Brenda! Don't move if you're in pain. Are you okay?" Brad crouched down next to her.

Brenda began to drag herself up slowly. She

wiped the snow off her face with short, angry flicks.

"Easy. Are you all right? Talk to me!" he urged.

"I'm fine," Brenda spat out disgustedly. A bolt of fiery anger shot through her. She would never live this down. The stings and aches that were scattered across her body were nothing compared to the damage to her ego.

Brad put his hand gently on her leg. "Move your foot for me. Come on."

Brenda rolled her eyes and tersely shook her foot. Her ski wobbled back and forth from the strap around her ankle. "I'm fine!"

"Now the other one."

Brenda shot him an angry glare. She was beginning to feel the chilling dampness soaking through her jeans and dripping down her face. Brad continued to stare at her with his worried, brown eyes.

"Move the other foot," he insisted.

Brenda complied. She knew nothing was broken. Slowly she unhooked her skis and stood up. Brad helped her attentively. As Brenda lifted her head, she got a sharp, bitter taste in her mouth and felt a wave of nausea.

Brad quickly stepped out of his own skis and put his arm around her. "Come on. Sit down for a few minutes."

He helped her over to the tree and Brenda leaned back. Her heart was still pumping like crazy. Brad fetched both pairs of skis, stuck them upright in the snow, and returned.

"Why didn't you tell me you don't ski that well?

You could have killed yourself." He was confused and obviously upset.

Brenda shrugged evasively. What was she supposed to say? I was scared to admit that I wasn't as good a skier as Chris. It was ridiculous. Just like the rest of her life, the whole situation was a disaster. She wanted them all just to leave her alone: Chris, Phoebe, Sasha, Brad — the whole lot.

"I'm serious," Brad warned. "People have had some brutal injuries on this hill. That was a really dumb thing to do."

"So," Brenda challenged, "it was my dumb thing to do, not yours! Don't worry about it."

"Why did you let me bring you up here? I never should have let you go down. I could tell when we got off the chair that you didn't know what you were doing."

"Look, it's not your fault, okay? You're not responsible for me. You've done your favor to Chris." Brenda angrily brushed the coating of snow off her sweater and pants. "Now why don't you just leave me alone?"

"What favor to Chris?" Brad demanded.

"Oh come on, I'm sure you wouldn't want to be seen even saying hello to me, let alone skiing with me. I know Chris asked you to take care of me."

"Chris didn't even tell me you were coming."

"Sure. Then why did you ski with me in the first place?"

Brad looked away and didn't answer. He took off his gloves and smacked them together.

"Look," Brenda said finally, "I appreciate your concern and help, but why don't you go back to your friends? I'm sure that's what you've been wanting to do all along. I just want to be left alone."

Brad was not leaving. "Why don't we just go down the rest of this slope together? There's another steep section coming up."

"Go on! I don't need taking care of. I just want to be left alone. Go back to your friends!"

Suddenly Brad exploded. "What makes you think I want to go back to my friends?" he shouted. "Do you think you're the only person in the world who feels out of it?"

Brenda was stunned. His outburst shocked her out of her own humiliation. She looked up at him with a startled expression. He didn't meet her eyes. For a few moments it was very quiet.

Finally Brad pressed the heel of his hand against his forehead. "I'm sorry, I'm in a lousy mood. It has nothing to do with you."

Brenda stared at him. "I'm sorry."

"No. It's me." He put his gloves back on. "Forget it."

"You were just trying to help me."

"I shouldn't have yelled at you. I'm sorry."

"It's all right," Brenda assured him softly. "I just act so dumb sometimes. It was my own fault."

"No, it was my fault. I should . . ." Brad stopped in the middle of his sentence and scratched the top of his head with his bulky glove. "This is absurd," he said with a hint of a smile.

Brenda felt the sides of her mouth curl up. "I'm a pro at creating absurd situations."

They shared one short, inaudible laugh. Brad

offered his hand to help Brenda up. As she took it, she noticed that he was shaking just a little. After she was on her feet, she held onto his hand for an extra second.

"Are you okay?" she asked.

He looked up at the perfect sky. "Absurd is just the right word for it. I've just been so out of it lately. None of the old stuff like my friends or school seems to make much sense." He smiled nervously. "Like I said, it's pretty absurd."

"I understand how that is," Brenda said slowly.

Their eyes met and Brenda felt a little self-conscious. She started to shake the snow out of her hair. He watched her.

"Do you feel better? You're not dizzy or anything, are you?"

"No. I'm fine."

"You look okay. Actually you look better than okay." He now had a soft look in his eyes that sent a tingle all the way through her.

"Yeah, sure." Brenda laughed. She retied her bandana and emptied the caked snow that was wedged in the cuffs of her jeans.

"How about a ski lesson?" Brad suggested suddenly.

Brenda hesitated, "Well. . . ."

"It can't be any worse than what just happened."

"I guess I could use a lesson."

"I think you can do the rest of this hill in a snowplow. You actually skied amazingly well considering how fast you were going."

"I have a way of doing things like that."

Brad and Brenda put their skis back on.

"There's an intermediate slope on the other side. Do you want to try that?"

Brenda nodded.

"Go on ahead of me," Brad urged warmly. "I'll be right behind you if you fall."

Chapter
6

"Pheeberooni!" hollered Woody as he carried a tray of food from the cafeteria line into the ski lodge dining room.

Phoebe looked up slowly, pushing her thick red hair away from her face. She sat at the table right next to the fireplace, the heat burning through her thick wool socks. She didn't care. She felt so cold that she wouldn't have cared if she'd caught on fire. She watched Woody's sweet face as he avoided stepping in a puddle of water and sat in the chair across from her.

"I'm glad I'm not the only one who had the sense to finally get out of the cold." He unloaded one chocolate bar, two doughnuts, a package of cookies, and a carton of milk from his tray. "Don't tell Sash." Woody smiled. "Maybe she can make it through the Arctic on nuts and seeds, but not me."

Phoebe picked up the chocolate bar. "Can I?" she asked listlessly.

Woody winked. "For you, Pheeberooni, anything."

Phoebe was glad that Woody had found her. He had always adored her, and she needed to be with somebody who felt that way, even if he wasn't the right somebody. She unwrapped the candy bar and began to eat.

"Where's everybody else?" Phoebe asked.

"Ted and Peter are hotdogging it down those killer runs. I decided to vote for self-preservation and bow out. If you see the patrol sled carting down two broken bodies, it's probably them." Woody opened his milk and took a huge swig. "I saw Sash on the way back. She was on the bunny slope giving pointers to Janie Barstow."

Phoebe hesitated before she spoke again. "Did you see Brad?" she managed finally in a thin voice.

Woody shook his head. "He must have gone off by himself."

"Yeah." Phoebe looked out the huge picture window. She still couldn't believe what she had seen that morning. Brad was obviously waiting for her outside the rental hut. But instead of approaching Phoebe, he had deliberately turned to Brenda and gone off with her. It was a cruel thing to do — to her and to Brenda. Phoebe couldn't help wondering if they were still skiing together.

"I guess Brenda went off alone, too, huh?" Phoebe hinted.

Woody was wolfing down the cookies. "Don't

know," he mumbled. "She's a strange one. Did she talk to you at all on the way up?"

"No." Phoebe shook her head. Of course, she hadn't said a word on the entire way up, either.

She continued to stare out the window, although she wasn't even sure what she was looking for. Brad. She was searching for his strong frame, his clear-cut, straightforward face. Yet it was more than that. She was searching for a time when things had been simpler and less painful, like when she and Brad had been together.

"Hey, Pheeb, no offense, but you've got that spacey, somewhere-over-the-rainbow look again."

Phoebe felt Woody's warm hand on hers. "Sorry. I've been like this a lot lately," she said quickly.

"Tell me about it. When Pheeberooni decides to come back down to earth, let me know. In the meantime, tell her I miss her."

Phoebe had to smile. She was lucky to have friends like Woody, especially after the whole mess with Brad and Griffin. Phoebe sat up straighter as a shaky breath tumbled through her.

"Pheeb?"

"What?"

"Have you heard anything more from Griffin?"

Phoebe raised her head sharply. At first she thought that Woody was reading her mind, but it was probably more obvious than that. Besides, Woody had been there when she and Griffin had gotten together, when she'd broken up with Brad, and when Griffin had left to be an actor in New York. If there was anybody who'd seen it all, it was Woody.

"No," she trembled. "I finally wrote him a letter. I just couldn't understand how he could break things off so quickly without explaining." Phoebe paused to take a deep breath. She could feel the pressure in her throat and wanted to avoid bursting into tears.

"And. . . ." Woody coaxed.

"It came back in the mail yesterday. Wrong address. Woody, I don't even know where he is now."

"Why don't you write him in care of the show?"

Phoebe sighed hopelessly. Sure, Griffin was acting in a Broadway show; maybe she could get a letter to him that way, but there was no point if he didn't want to see her.

That thought made Phoebe cold again, and she moved even closer to the fire. It was over with Griffin. She had to face it; there was no choice. All she could wish was that life could go back to normal, to the way it was before Griffin had come into her life, back when she had been with Brad.

Woody seemed to sense her confusion. "I think there's one very important thing that you have to do."

"What's that?" Phoebe asked gratefully.

"Come outside and help me build the best snowman this mountain has ever seen."

Phoebe looked up into Woody's loving face. His thick brows were knitted together with concern and affection. She gathered her gloves, hat, and scarf.

"Okay," Phoebe said. Anything to take her mind off of Griffin and Brad. She snapped one of

Woody's suspenders and let him lead the way outside.

Sasha handed her skis back to the man at the rental hut and sat down to take off Woody's sister's boots. She finally had left Janie to figure out the rope tow on her own, then headed back to return her equipment. The sun was disappearing, her ears were starting to burn, and somehow her feet had gotten wet. At least she had an extra pair of socks in her backpack.

After changing her socks, Sasha stood up and took a few steps. Without the heavy boots and skis, her legs felt so light it was like walking on the moon. She began to giggle as she marched weightlessly around on the old indoor-outdoor carpet. It was a wonderful feeling, although her muscles were so tired she couldn't quite keep her balance.

"Whoa, foxette," called a loud, deep voice. Before Sasha could turn around and see John Marquette's fleshy face, she felt his thick arm pull her back on the wooden bench. Marquette immediately plopped down next to her.

"Oooh, you are such a little fox." Marquette leered, attempting to put his arm around her.

Sasha tried to control her annoyance. Phrases like "little fox" made her cringe, but she knew Marquette was too dumb to realize how offensive he was being. She jerked her shoulder, causing him to take his arm away.

"I was looking for you all day," he said.

"I was on the beginners' slope."

Marquette shrugged. "I guess that's why I didn't see you. I just couldn't tear myself away from those monster hills."

Sasha almost laughed out loud. Marquette was a great football player and wrestler, but she had seen him take off on skis after they'd rented their equipment. He was even more inept on the slopes than she was.

"Oh, really?" she challenged. "Did you race Ted? Too bad Chris wasn't here. I bet you could have even shown her up." Sasha's voice dripped with sarcasm.

Marquette shifted uncomfortably. "Yeah, well," he cleared his throat. "Listen, foxette."

Sasha gritted her teeth.

"I wanted to talk to you about the newspaper."

Sasha felt a wave of relief. At least it was the newspaper he was after, not her.

"My cousin saw that big article you did."

Sasha had to sit up and listen when Marquette mentioned his cousin. He was the owner of Super-jock, the biggest independent sporting goods store in Washington, and an important advertiser for *The Red and the Gold.* "What big article?"

"The one about Tim Neary, that cross-country wimp."

"What about it?"

Marquette scrunched up his face. "Why did you do an article about a pathetic guy like that?"

"Tim set a new record, that's why." Sasha worked to maintain her self-control.

"Well, I set plenty of records, too. So how come you haven't done an article about me?"

"Because I have other things to write about."

Sasha couldn't believe Marquette's nerve, although she had heard that he was an egomaniac. And she had seen the blown-up picture of himself taped inside his hall locker.

"Who do you have to write about who's better than me? Pansies like Neary? More dumb articles about those drama skits your wimp friend Woody puts on?" Marquette let loose with a deep throaty laugh. "What a joke that guy is."

Anger raced through Sasha. She pulled on her borrowed boots and stood up. "I wouldn't put down Woody if I were you," she said, letting her temper take over.

Marquette stood up, too. He towered over her. "Oh yeah? You got a thing for him? That's too bad. He's the worst excuse for a guy that I've ever seen."

"Oh, really?" Sasha challenged. "As a matter of fact, I don't have a thing for him, but I'm still sure that —"

"That what?"

"That Woody Webster is ten times more of a man than you are, and do you want to know why?"

"Why?"

"Because he doesn't have to prove it all the time, that's why!"

Marquette paused for a minute. Sasha wasn't sure if what she had said had affected him, or if he just didn't understand it. But to drive the point home, she went on. "If you were really such a big man you wouldn't have to bully people all the time and call girls degrading names and drive that gross car. That's what I think!"

Her voice rang with passion and was answered by two pairs of clapping hands. Sasha saw Ted and Peter standing in the doorway.

"Hey, you tell him, Sasha," Peter said.

"Can't win them all, Marquette," Ted added.

Marquette was turning red with rage. He stood like an overheated boiler, staring back and forth between the guys and Sasha.

There was a short, tense pause.

Finally Marquette scooped up his parka and turned back to Sasha. "You just wait, foxette," he threatened. "You're going to beg me for an interview. And when you do, it'll be on my terms."

He stormed out, shoving between Peter and Ted as he went through the door. The guys watched him go before sauntering over to Sasha.

"Way to go, Sash." Ted smiled.

"That'll teach him to pick on people who are smaller than he is," joked Peter.

Sasha grinned proudly. She wasn't afraid of a bully like Marquette. But she wasn't entirely sure he had understood anything she had said.

Chapter
7

"You have jelly on your chin."

"I do not."

"Want to bet?" Brad gently ran his hand along Brenda's chin. Victoriously he held up a finger covered with thick purple doughnut filling. Brenda started to giggle.

"I don't think my mouth is working right. It's too cold." She shivered. They were the first two back in the bus, and Brenda's teeth were chattering. She had fallen so many times on the slopes that her clothes were soaked to her skin. "How come you never fall down? That's what I want to know." Brenda took another big bite of her jelly doughnut. Again the filling dribbled down her face. They both burst out laughing.

Brenda wasn't sure why it was so easy to laugh all of a sudden. Somehow, after her ridiculous stunt on the green run, it seemed like nothing worse could happen. Brad had already seen what a fool she was, and instead of snubbing her, he seemed to like her better for it.

Brad slid a little closer and huddled against her. "I didn't fall," he began gaily, pulling another doughnut from the white paper bag, "because I was trying to prove to you what a great guy I am."

As he took his first bite, a huge blob of jelly squirted out the bottom and onto the cuff of his sweater. "See," he laughed, holding up his wrist, "aren't you impressed?"

Brenda helped mop his cuff with a paper napkin. "These things are dangerous." She laughed. The napkin was glued by the jelly to Brad's sweater.

"You should have seen me last year. I let your stepsister talk me into a downhill race. I creamed out about halfway down and she just whizzed on by." Brad gave half his doughnut to Brenda. "What was really dumb was that I was actually kind of mad about it."

"Chris probably made you mad. She would race down the slope." Brenda couldn't hide the trace of bitterness in her voice.

"It wasn't Chris's fault. I just used to be so hung up on that kind of stuff — being the best at everything, never losing, getting into the best college, heading the most school clubs, you know." He offered Brenda an embarrassed shrug in explanation. "But I'm beginning to think a lot of that stuff isn't so important anymore." He fastened the bus window and slid it down. Leaning way out, he tossed the crumpled paper bag toward a nearby trash can. It missed. "See?" He laughed as he got up and walked out of the bus.

Brenda slid over to Brad's empty place and leaned through the window frame. She watched him jog along the snowy lot, pick up the bag, and toss it into the can. When he came back to meet her at the window, he lightly stamped his feet and rubbed his hands together.

"You know what?" Brad smiled. "It's cold out here." His face was very close to hers.

"Well, come on back in," Brenda teased as she pulled up the window and waited for him to return to the inside of the bus. Brenda had suggested waiting in the bus rather than the lodge. She didn't want to be around all the other people, and Brad hadn't objected. She wondered if he was relieved not to be seen with her. She would find out soon enough, when everybody else returned.

Brad hurried back onto the bus and sat down next to her. He grabbed her hands and started rubbing his own against them for warmth. "Brrr. Your hands are so warm."

Then he stopped and looked her in the face. Brenda felt a sudden flush, as if the bus's thermostat had just been cranked up, then a wave of self-consciousness. It became very quiet and Brad released her hands. He shifted a little nervously as if he couldn't find a comfortable position for his tall fame. Finally he was still, facing her with one foot up on the bus seat, arms wrapped around his knee. There was a new seriousness in his face.

"What is it with you and Chris?" he asked. "How come I've never talked to you before? You've been at Kennedy — what, a year? — and nobody knows you."

Brenda looked at her lap and pulled her cuffs over her hands. "Everybody knows me too well."

"What do you mean?"

"At school, they know all the bad stuff and that's all they want to know."

"You mean about how you ran away?"

Brenda nodded. She was feeling very uncomfortable, but Brad didn't seem to want to let the subject drop.

"Everybody at school knows that you ran away and stayed at that house in D.C., but I don't think people care that much. It was after your mom remarried, right?"

"Yeah."

"I guess that was pretty upsetting."

Brenda didn't know how much to say. She'd never talked about this with anyone at Kennedy before. "It was a lot of things."

There was a long pause. Brad was obviously waiting for her to explain. "Moving, a new school, I didn't get along with my stepfather or Chris. I was in the same history class as Chris and she always did well. I felt like such a jerk compared to her, so I guess I cut too many times."

"Did they call your folks and all that?"

Brenda cleared her throat. "Yeah. My stepfather went nuts. We had this huge fight, and I couldn't believe it when my mother took his side. Maybe that was what did it. I felt like she'd deserted me. I just felt like nobody cared."

Brenda looked over at Brad. His warm eyes were totally focused on her. "It's hard when somebody you depend on deserts you. It kind of makes you angry at the whole world. I know."

Brenda assumed that Brad was referring to the break-up with Phoebe, but she didn't know much about it and didn't quite know how to ask.

"Anyway," she said instead, "I spend a lot of time working with kids down at Garfield House, the place where I went when I ran away. You know, helping them and stuff, so I don't have much time for a school social life."

"I bet you're really good at that, helping kids, stuff like that."

"Why?"

"I can just tell." Brad was about to say something else when they both saw a pack of tired skiers trudging towards the bus. Instinctively, Brenda moved so she wasn't so close to him. A warning bell had just gone off inside her. Sure, something was developing between her and Brad, but just wait and see how he acted with other people around.

The first pair of bedraggled kids entered the bus. Brenda didn't know them, but they waved hello to Brad, gave her a funny look, and wearily sat down. When Ted and Peter entered they both stared a little too long, but at least they tried to be subtle. As the others straggled back, they gave Brenda confused stares, said hello to Brad, and took their seats. Woody Webster was actually rendered silent. Even Janie Barstow took an extra moment to pause and gawk. Brenda fidgeted nervously, but the reactions didn't seem to faze Brad. If anything, he was leaning closer to her, making it obvious to everyone that he liked her.

Brenda sat forward when she saw Sasha walk dreamily down the aisle.

"Hi!" Sasha beamed, finally seeing Brenda. "You disappeared so fast this morning, I didn't know where you went. Did you have a good time?" Sasha was the first person who hadn't reacted to Brenda's being with Brad.

"Yeah," Brenda answered gratefully.

Sasha stepped into the seat and tugged the sunglasses that hung around Brad's neck. "I used that sunscreen you told me about. I don't think I got burned." She poked an index finger along her porcelain cheek. "I get these terminal sunburns," she explained to Brenda.

"How was your lesson?" Brenda asked shyly.

"Good! I went all the way to the top of the beginner slope. Oh, guess what? You know that comp we have to do for Barnes?"

Brenda nodded.

"I finally thought of an idea for it when I was on the slope. Now I'll have to pull an all-nighter to write it."

Brenda was about to question Sasha about her essay when she noticed Phoebe. She was standing behind Sasha, staring directly at Brenda and Brad. Brad had turned to talk with Barry Moss, a senior sitting behind him. Finally Phoebe turned and slipped into the front seat.

As the bus rumbled down the mountain, Brenda saw frequent head turns in her direction. Only Sasha, who was scribbling madly in a small notebook, seemed not to care. Phoebe was the most interested one of them all.

Brenda was amazed that Brad never let the attention bother him. He was open and demonstrative about his newfound affection. When she started to feel tired, he encouraged her to lean her head on his shoulder and even made a pillow for her from an extra sweater.

Brenda was trying to stay cool, but she was beginning to be overwhelmed by her feelings and by Brad's physical nearness. When she started to shiver, Brad wrapped both arms around her. She felt the warmth of his chest, the slight coarseness of his sweater against her face. Brenda imagined she was sliding into a wonderful, warm pool. She had to close her eyes, because she was afraid that everyone would know exactly what was going on inside her.

By the time the bus pulled into the Kennedy parking lot it was almost dark. As the vehicle grumbled to a halt, Brenda rose and gathered her belongings. The group filed slowly off the bus, with Brad close behind Brenda.

"Well, bye," Brenda said shyly as she stepped out. Brad immediately took her hand and led her a few feet away from the others. Then Brenda noticed Phoebe. She was standing not far away next to her station wagon, staring at Brad and Brenda almost as if she wanted them to see her.

"Brenda, are you ready to go?" Phoebe finally called in a hard voice.

Brad whispered to Brenda before she could answer. "I'll call you, okay?"

"Okay," Brenda managed. "Bye." She headed over to Phoebe's car.

"I'll call you!" Brad yelled again. He waved happily.

When Brenda reached the car, Phoebe had just ducked into the driver's seat. As soon as Brenda pulled her door shut, Phoebe started the engine and pulled out of the lot. She didn't say a word, but even in the dim twilight Brenda could see the tension in her pretty face.

Phoebe turned the radio on loudly. This time she didn't sing along with it. She stared ahead at the traffic and gripped the steering wheel. The short ride to Brenda's home seemed to take forever.

Finally Phoebe pulled into the driveway and Brenda stared to get out.

Phoebe's voice stopped her. "Brenda," she began forcefully.

"Yes?"

"I don't know quite how to say this." Phoebe hesitated. "I just don't want to see you hurt."

"What is it?"

"You should know that . . . when you went off to ski with Brad . . . it was because I was standing there watching."

"So?"

"Brenda." Phoebe's voice had a low, no-nonsense tone to it. "He's only paying attention to you to make me jealous."

The world around Brenda stopped for a minute. "What?"

Phoebe leaned over the steering wheel, her thick red hair hiding her face. "Brad saw me standing outside the rental place and then he turned around and went up to you. I'm sorry, but it's just so obvious. I don't want to let him drag you into his immature attempt to hurt me."

An awful, tight feeling constricted Brenda's chest, so that it was almost hard to breath. Her first reaction was that Phoebe was out to hurt *her* for some reason. But then she felt Phoebe's hand on her arm. Brenda turned to face her.

"I'm sure he doesn't mean to hurt you," Phoebe added, finally showing her melancholy face. "Things are just kind of complicated between him and me."

Brenda gathered all her self-control and responded, "I understand." She tried not to slam the car door, but she heard it crash shut just before she reached the front door to the house.

Chapter
8

Brenda ran up the hall stairs two at a time. Phoebe's words were playing over and over in her head. Brad was just using Brenda. If it were true, everyone else had probably known exactly what was going on. It made Brenda feel sick. Once she hit the top stair she pulled herself around by the banister and raced into her room, shutting the door behind her and falling, gear and all, onto her bed.

Immediately she heard footsteps out in the hall — then her sister's cheery voice. Chris had been waiting for her.

"Bren? Brenda?" Chris called through the bedroom door. "You home? How was it?"

For a moment Brenda didn't answer. She couldn't. Every muscle in her body was tied up.

"I'm tired. I'll talk to you later," she finally managed, her voice shaky and raw. She waited until she heard Chris walk back down the hall to her own room.

Brenda turned over on the bed, arms wide, face to the wall. Now that she thought about it, she recalled seeing Phoebe at the rental hut when Brad had asked her to ski with him. How could she have been so stupid? That *was* why Brad had suddenly turned so friendly. Brenda had been too preoccupied with her skis at the time to contemplate it. But now that she thought back to that morning on the bus, she felt like a total fool. Of course Brad was still hung up on Phoebe.

And the whole ugly charade on the way home. No wonder Brad hadn't reacted to the stares they got. He could afford to be cool, because like everybody else, he knew exactly why he was talking to Brenda. He wanted to be affectionate and warm with her — but just for that one trip. That was exactly the point. Make a big show so your old girl friend gets jealous and comes crawling back.

Brenda made herself stand up and change her clothes. Her jeans were still damp in the creases, and the legs were a little stiff. She peeled off her tights — the toes were still icy. Brenda pulled her bathrobe off the hook in her closet and headed for the shower.

As she shoved open her bedroom door, Brenda almost pushed over a surprised Chris, who was just raising her hand to knock on the other side. Brenda's stepsister had her hair in a high ponytail and wore a velour pullover and white jeans. Chris was still sniffing, but looked much pinker and brighter than the night before.

Brenda tried to act as if nothing was wrong. She made herself keep it together.

Chris was too excited to notice. "Bren," bubbled Chris, "Brad Davidson is on the phone for you! I talked to him for a few minutes already. He said you two skied together and he had a really good time." She barely paused for a breath. "That's so great! I haven't heard him sound this happy since before he and Phoebe broke up."

Brenda turned toward the bathroom. "Tell him I'm not here."

"What?"

"I'm not home. Okay?"

Chris looked mystified. "I'll be right back."

Chris walked back to her room and Brenda headed into the bathroom. A moment later there was a short knock, and Chris stepped in. Brenda tried to ignore her. She turned the hot water on full blast and let the steam fill the tiny room. Her shoulder was beginning to ache, and she was shivering again.

Chris hiked herself up onto the counter. She watched her stepsister as Brenda busily gathered towels, soap, and shampoo. Brenda avoided her gaze.

"Brad left his phone number. He asked you to call him back." Chris crossed her legs and tapped them against the wooden cabinets.

Brenda brushed her hair. It was knotted and unusually curly from the snow and wind. She wiped away a circle in the steamy mirror and looked at her face. Her cheeks were rosy from the sun, and there were tiny smudges of makeup under her dark eyes.

"Brenda," Chris insisted finally, "do you want to tell me what's going on? Brad happens to be a very nice guy. He's student body —"

"— president," Brenda said at the same time. "Who cares?"

"I just mean that he's not some nerd. I don't understand you sometimes."

"That's for sure." Brenda waited for Chris to move toward the door, but it was clear that her sister wanted the conversation to continue. She reached into the shower and turned the water off, then leaned over the sink and began to wash her face.

"So how was it up at Jackson?" Chris asked. "Did you have an okay time at least?"

"No," Brenda said into the sink, "I had an awful time, just like I thought I would. I don't like those people and they don't like me. Okay?" Brenda reached blindly for a towel. Chris handed her one.

"Did anything happen?"

"No."

"I can't believe Sasha and Phoebe weren't nice."

Brenda hesitated. "They're okay."

"But why did Brad call and say he had a good time with you?"

Brenda shrugged and the towel fell onto the floor. "Look, I know you wanted me to go and have the most wonderful day of my life, but I didn't. So let's just drop the whole thing, okay?"

Chris slid off the counter to pick up Brenda's towel and hang it on the rack. She looked guilty and disappointed. "I'm sorry. I thought —"

"I know," Brenda sighed. She did know that

Chris meant well, that she was really trying to help. It was just that everything Chris pushed her into turned into some kind of disaster.

Neither of them said anything for a few seconds. Chris started to leave but stopped at the door. "Oh, at least there's some good news. I have a surprise for you." She tried to smile.

"What?"

"Well, since I knew I kind of trapped you into going on the ski trip, I typed your paper for you. The one for Barnes. It's on my desk."

Brenda looked up with a start. Her essay about Tony Martinez? That was not intended to be read by Chris or anyone else in her family. Chris should have left it alone. Brenda almost told her so, but Chris was looking at her with such expectation. Brenda didn't want to disappoint her stepsister again.

"Thanks. That's a big help."

Chris smiled. "That essay was really good. Honest, Bren. I thought it was moving and well written. It was better than most of the stuff I read in magazines."

"Sure."

"It was. I wouldn't say it if I didn't think it was true. You should send it in to the school paper or something."

Brenda cringed at the suggestion but tried not to let Chris see. "Right."

"Anyway, at least you won't have to spend tomorrow at the typewriter. Maybe you can go visit Garfield House."

Garfield House was exactly where Brenda was going. "Chris, I've got to get into the shower.

Thanks for doing my paper. Sorry about the ski trip."

"Me, too." Chris closed the door behind her.

Brenda stepped into the shower and leaned one arm and her forehead against the tiles. She turned the water on. It began rolling down her back. She took a deep breath as the water warmed her body. Tears began to slide down her cheeks.

Chapter 9

"So nothing weird happened to Brenda on the ski trip?" asked Chris as she hopped onto the corner of Sasha's desk. Her nose was red, and she coughed as she spoke.

Sasha took the pencil out of her mouth and stuck it in the base of her thick braid. "Not as far as I could tell. She and Brad looked really into each other on the bus on the way home."

"That's what Ted said. I don't get it." Chris pushed up the sleeves of her yellow sweater and took the scissors from the desk-top. Nervously she snapped the blades open and closed.

"Chris, put those scissors down. You're going to cut off your fingers. I don't want blood all over my ad copy. Even I'm not that organic."

Chris laughed and then sighed. "Sorry."

It was Monday after school and the girls sat in the journalism room. They were alone except for Mr. Kulp, the teacher who was in charge of *The*

Red and the Gold. He was holed up in his tiny office at the other end of the room.

"I thought Brad was acting like he really liked her."

"That's what I thought when I talked to him on the phone. You know what I think it might be?"

"What?" Sasha removed the pencil from her hair and made a note on one of the papers scattered before her. Her hands were covered with typewriter ink and correction fluid.

"I think that Brad does really like her but that Brenda is just too insecure to believe it. She needs to get more confidence in herself."

"Well, what can you do about that?"

"I don't know." Chris frowned. She sniffed and opened her notebook on the desk. With great purpose, she unclipped some carbon-copied papers from the immaculate inside cover. "Take a look at this and tell me what you think."

Sasha looked up curiously as Chris slid the stapled stack of papers in front of her. When she saw what it was, her brown eyes opened wide. "This is Brenda's essay for Barnes's English class. Did she give it to you?"

"Are you kidding? I typed it for her and stuck a carbon in. Just read it and give me your professional opinion. Okay?"

"Sure." Sasha shrugged. She put her hands over her ears, leaned forward, and began to read with total concentration.

A few minutes later Sasha was still poring over the pages, but Chris couldn't help interrupting. "Is it as good as I think it is?"

Sasha waved her hand without looking up. "Wait a sec, Chris. Let me finish."

Finally Sasha turned over the last page and raised her head. Her eyes were damp.

"Well?"

"It's terrific."

Chris jumped off the desk and clapped her hands together. "That's what I thought! I can't believe she isn't going to show this essay to my dad. He'd go crazy, he'd be so proud of her."

"She's going to get an A from Barnes, that's for sure," Sasha marveled. "All that stuff about that Martinez guy and the halfway house is really great. This is better than ninety percent of the junk that goes in the paper."

Chris nodded excitedly. "I know! After I read it over, I decided to put a carbon in when I typed it, you know, because I thought maybe I'd show my dad so he wouldn't be so hard on her. But then I thought of something even better. Since you think it's good, too, how about showing it to Mr. Kulp?"

"What for?"

Chris took a big breath. "I thought if Kulp read it maybe he'd ask her to write something for the paper. I don't know. I just thought if she did something like that, maybe she'd feel better about herself, have more confidence. I know my dad would love it if she had an article in the paper."

Sasha looked skeptical. "Isn't it kind of weird to do this and not tell Brenda?"

"It is weird. I agree, it is definitely weird. But what else am I supposed to do? She says no to everything I suggest."

Sasha paused to look over the papers again. She shook her head. "This is really good. It's a waste for just Barnes to see it. He's so cool, he'll probably just pat her on the head and act like it's no big deal."

"That's right. So how about if we show it to Kulp and explain to him about Brenda and her problems and all —"

Sasha jumped in passionately. "And see if Kulp will pretend like he heard about the essay from Barnes, and then ask her to write something for the paper!"

"Yes! That's perfect!"

Sasha jumped up at the same time that Chris took a step forward. They almost tumbled into each other, but quickly regained their composure. Both were eyeing the door to Mr. Kulp's office. With conspiratorial smiles, Sasha and Chris walked to the teacher's tiny room. Sasha knocked on the door.

"Come in," Mr. Kulp called gruffly. He was stooped over a long table covered with photographs. He looked tired. As the girls entered, he took off his glasses and rubbed his eyes. "Sasha, I was just going to come out and talk to you," he said before either of the girls had a chance to speak. He was pushing the photos around on the table top.

"Yes, Mr. Kulp?"

"We've got a problem for the next issue," he continued, cleaning his glasses with the corner of his sweater.

"What?"

"I've got half my staff out with this flu that's

going around." He looked up suddenly. "You're okay, aren't you?" he asked Sasha, obviously afraid he might be losing his star reporter, too.

"Don't worry. I took about five vitamin C's today."

Mr. Kulp gave her an amused smile. "Of course." He slipped his glasses back on and seemed to notice Chris for the first time. "Chris, what are you doing here? Want to write something for the next issue?" he asked jokingly.

"I don't think so. We wanted to ask you —"

Mr. Kulp was much too concerned with his own situation to listen. "We've got the layout all ready for the coming issue. I've been waiting for Patty Slover's article, the one on the SAT scores — and I just got a note from the office saying she's too sick to do any work and won't be back for at least a week. So, what do we do?" He looked back down at the photos.

Chris took a step forward. "You mean you need something for this coming issue?" Her eyes were gleaming. She looked back at Sasha, who answered her excited look with a smile.

"I sure do," Kulp groaned. "Sasha, do you have any old pieces lying around that you've been wanting to print?"

Chris was practically bouncing on her toes. She touched Sasha on the arm as if to urge her to speak.

Sasha tapped Brenda's paper against the door frame. "Mr. Kulp, I have a great essay right here by a new writer. How about that?"

He gave Sasha a look of relief. "Fine with me. If you think it's good enough, put it in. You know

I trust your judgment. Patty's space was for six hundred words. Just get the new piece to me as soon as you can."

Sasha glanced one last time at Chris to see if her friend really wanted to go through with it. Chris nodded yes in one clear, strong gesture. "Yes, Mr. Kulp," Sasha said.

"Good. Now clear out of here so I can figure out the rest of this mess. Chuck Couch took the advertising records home with him and I can't figure out what's what. Two of these photos are out of focus. . . ."

Mr. Kulp continued to ramble as the girls backed out of his office. As soon as Chris had closed his office door, she threw her arms around Sasha.

"This is great!" Sasha assured her.

"I don't believe it!"

"That essay is so good, I'm telling you —"

"I can't wait to see my dad's face. He's going to love it!"

"I can't wait to see Brenda's face!"

Suddenly the celebration stopped and Chris looked at Sasha more soberly.

"Do you think she'll mind?" Sasha asked.

Chris hesitated before breaking into a proud smile. "That's just the chance we have to take."

Chapter 10

"Hey, baby! You all by yourself?"

Brenda frowned as a guy hanging off the end of a newpaper delivery van winked at her. It was Sunday morning, and she was at the edge of Georgetown. Except for the delivery man and her, nobody was on the street. Brenda walked quickly, fists shoved into her jacket pockets, black beret planted securely on top of her head, scarf wrapped high around her neck. The delivery man continued to taunt her, but she ignored him.

Jumping over a deep puddle, Brenda crossed the street. She passed a parking lot, some boardinghouses for college students, and a chain link fence bent on its side. After a right turn, she was walking into a more residential area, one marked by small, historical townhouses. In the middle of the block stood Garfield House — a narrow three story building that was slightly rundown, but it had two young trees sprouting in front near the sidewalk. Brenda dashed up the porch and went in.

"Brenda! My favorite girl!"

Inside the hallway Brenda found herself engulfed by a big, enthusiastic hug. She was surrounded by an army field jacket and curly hair as she was literally lifted off her feet to the sound of a deep, warm laugh. She began laughing as well, slapping her captor on the back.

"Hey, Tony!" she yelled.

"Hey, pal!" Tony yelled back.

"Hey, Tony!" Brenda yelled again.

They both laughed some more as Tony set her back on the floor and stood back to look at her.

"How ya doin'?" He spoke with a slight Spanish accent.

Seeing her old friend was already making Brenda feel better. Nineteen-year-old Tony was the big brother she never had: supportive, wise, warm, and safe. "I'm all right." She giggled and threw a mock punch at him. "How about you?"

Immediately Tony crouched in a playful fighting position. He was a weight lifter and amateur boxer. Brenda thought his muscles were too much, but she had to admit he was strong. She'd once seen him relocate the Garfield House Coke machine all by himself.

"I'm hanging in there. Keeping in shape." Tony faked her out with a punch and threw his arm around her shoulder, patting the top of her head. Suddenly his face grew more serious, and he lowered his voice. "I'm glad you're here. I have to talk to you about something important before you go."

"Okay," Brenda responded instantly. Tony led her into the main floor living room. There were a half dozen kids in a circle waiting for him. "We're just starting a rap session. You stay with Carla. You've been doing great with her."

Brenda nodded enthusiastically. Carla was the special girl Brenda had been working with the last few weeks. At fifteen, Carla had run away three times since her parents' divorce and had adopted Garfield House as her home away from home. She also had a serious habit of cutting school, but with Brenda's help she was making progress.

Brenda joined the small circle, giving Carla a friendly smile. Tony sat down, too, and began the session.

"Okay guys, we have an important person here. Some of you know Brenda Austin. She was here just like you only a year ago. But she's back home and doing better in school. Everything's not perfect, but she's taking steps. Right?" He took off his army jacket and smiled at her.

Brenda nodded. Things were a lot better than they had been last year. She just had to think of the last few days as a minor setback.

Tony leaned forward on his elbows. "Carla, since Brenda's here, why don't we start with you? I know that you two have been talking about stuff at school. How was the last week for you?"

Carla shrugged evasively, her sad eyes staring down at the ancient green carpet.

"Did you cut?" Tony insisted.

"Just one day," Carla admitted toughly. She drew her legs up under her and hunched over them. "Just Friday. I went to my first class and I answered this question wrong and it was like everybody was going to laugh at me. The teacher just made this snide comment like I'm dumb or something. I don't have to take that."

"I hear you, Carla. Brenda, what do you have to say to her?"

Brenda responded immediately. "How about a grounding exercise?"

Tony stretched back in his chair, his thick arms folded over his chest. "Go ahead."

"You ready, Carla?" Brenda asked.

Carla turned to face her. "Yeah."

"Okay. If you go to school and everybody does laugh at you, what's going to happen?"

Carla shifted. "I'll know they all think I'm a fool."

"Okay." Brenda scooted up to the edge of her chair. "If everybody thinks you're a fool, then what?"

"Then nobody wants to talk to me or be my friend."

"If nobody wants to be your friend what happens?"

"Then I guess I'm all alone."

A few kids started to laugh. Carla joined them.

Tony broke in. "Wait. It's not so ridiculous. Brenda, you finish grounding for Carla."

Brenda nodded. "Okay. If people think you're a fool, then they won't like you, no one will talk to you, you won't have any friends. Then you will be really lonely and go crazy from loneliness. Then if you get sick or something no one would help you, not even a doctor would treat you. And so you'd die."

Everybody was laughing now. They always did when they went through a grounding exercise. That was the point, to show how people often reacted to small incidents as if they were life-threatening. The exercise was supposed to "ground" them, put things in perspective.

"Sure it's funny," Tony took control again, "but think about it. Cutting a lot of school is serious. You've got to have a major reason to do it. Subconsciously Carla probably feels that going to school really is life-threatening, or she wouldn't spend so much energy figuring ways to cut. Maybe if you realize it's not so dangerous, you can face it better. All of you try a grounding exercise next time you feel threatened. If your life is at stake that's one thing, but if you're acting like your life is at stake just because people might laugh at you, then that's dumb." Tony looked over at Brenda and grinned. "Good work."

Tony went on to a tall, dark-haired boy, but Brenda didn't really pay attention. Working with Carla made her think about her own reaction to Brad and Phoebe. Yes, she had been used. Yes, she had developed feelings for Brad only to find out that he didn't really care for her. But it didn't mean the world was coming to an end, and she shouldn't act like it had. Just walking in and seeing the kids at the house and the hurt in their eyes made Brenda put her own problems in better perspective. Finally the session was over and the group started to break up. Tony motioned Brenda over. "Let's go to my office."

Brenda nodded and followed Tony down the

hall, past the Coke machine and brightly painted water pipes to his office near the back.

Tony's office was a little bigger than a large closet. There was just space for a desk, which was covered with papers and books, a small set of dumbbells, and two armless chairs.

"Have a seat." Brenda sat on one of the metal kitchen chairs.

Tony squeezed in behind his desk and began searching for something under the mess on top. "I got something real important to talk to you about, but before we get into it, how's things?" he asked quickly. "Everything basically okay?"

Brenda hesitated. She'd felt like explaining to Tony all that had happened to her in the last couple of days — the disaster of the ski trip, how Chris kept pushing her at Kennedy. But now she thought she could handle it herself. Besides, Tony looked like he had something crucial to discuss. "No major problems," Brenda answered.

"Good." Tony folded his hands on top of his desk and looked at her. For the first time, Brenda noticed that there was a little bit of worry in his face.

"A fourteen-year-old girl named Julie Meeker ran away Friday night," Tony began. "Some guy at the twenty-four hour deli near Dupont Circle called me yesterday. What happened was Julie came in and talked to this guy who works the counter at night. Julie told him that she couldn't go home and had no money. She asked him if he knew a place for her to go, but this guy didn't know what to tell her. Anyway, some other creep came up to Julie and said he wanted to help her. So Julie went with him and was last seen getting into his car."

"Oh no," Brenda gasped.

Tony was shaking his head. "So this guy finally told Casey, the owner, about Julie and what happened. Casey called me yesterday. Me and a couple of the kids here were out almost all last night looking for her." Tony frowned and threw up his hand. "But nothing."

"What can I do to help?" Brenda knew she would do anything to get that girl off the street.

"I don't know what more we can do about Julie, except look for her. The cops have all the info. It just shouldn't have happened in the first place. She should have known we were here and come to us first thing. What good are we if kids like Julie don't know where to go?"

Brenda recalled how lucky she'd been to have Tony find her in that twenty-four hour coffee shop the night she ran away. She had been sitting there since three in the afternoon because she didn't have enough money to pay for the greasy hamburger she'd eaten. By then it was almost midnight, and she could barely stay awake, and that weird guy with the beard kept approaching her and asking if she needed a ride somewhere. But Brenda would have stayed in that diner all week to avoid the humiliation of crawling back home after that horrendous fight with her stepfather. She didn't want to think about what might have happened if the cashier hadn't called Tony and Tony hadn't talked her into going to Garfield House.

"Here's where I need your help. I'm starting a big campaign to get the word out to every high school and junior high in the area."

"Good idea."

"Yeah. You're the only one I know at Kennedy. I want to do it quick. Can you arrange for me to speak to a group there? Maybe the student council, something like that. I can give them the facts and then you can follow through and see that word gets around to the whole school."

Brenda looked up with alarm. Going to the student council! There was only one person she knew who could help her with that, and he was the last person she wanted to see, let alone talk to. The thought of asking a favor of Brad Davidson made her want to get up and run from Tony's office.

"Brenda, is there a problem?" Tony asked when she didn't respond.

Brenda pushed a layer of hair away from her face and thought about the grounding exercise. What would happen when she looked Brad in the face again?

She would feel hurt, and he would know how she felt about him. If Brad knew how she felt, he could use her again to get Phoebe back and she would hurt so much she might get crazy and run away again. Then she would slide back after all the progress she had made over the last year and — she would die.

Brenda didn't even crack a smile at the results of her grounding exercise. The end didn't seem as ridiculous as it did with Carla. It seemed all too real.

"Brenda." Tony looked at her intently. "Can you handle it?"

Brenda thought about Julie Meeker trying to get along by herself. Brad Davidson suddenly didn't seem like a big deal. If there was one thing Brenda could really do, it was help other kids who had problems.

"I can handle it," Brenda heard herself saying to Tony.

"Are you sure?"

"Absolutely."

Tony leaned forward in his chair, a big smile on his face. "Great. I knew I could count on you."

Chapter
11

"Did you guys see that concert on MTV last night?"

Woody was sitting across from Chris, lining up pomegranate seeds on a paper napkin. Chris hoped that he wasn't preparing to launch them at Ted with his thumb.

"I saw part of it," Ted responded. "I didn't think it was so hot."

Woody shook his head. "Me, either. In fact, I actually turned it off and went back to doing my homework. Can you believe that?"

"Woody, what are you doing with those seeds?" Chris interrupted.

"Yeah," Sasha said, reaching over and plucking one up from the napkin, "you should eat them. They're good for you."

"Don't do that!" Woody exclaimed, a look of mock horror coming over his large, open features. "Now look, you've ruined my chorus line."

"Your chorus line?"

"Yeah, I was staging my new Broadway musical. It was a pomegranate seed chorus line. They were going to dance."

Chris sighed. Some days she just couldn't follow Woody, and it was turning out to be one of those days. In fact, the whole lunchroom scene was proving to be a little too much. Peter was playing a lot of heavy metal music over the school radio station, and it was blaring right down from the speaker over the crowd's table. Phoebe had been moping all day, hardly saying a word to Chris and refusing to tell her why. Chris's cold still lingered, although it had definitely gotten better over the weekend. Ted was the only person who kept her steady. He was there as usual, right at her side, teasing Woody and occasionally flashing reassuring looks her way.

"Do you know we're starting jazz dance next week in p.e.?" Sasha asked after gobbling up most of Woody's chorus line. "Phoebe, I bet you'll be good at that."

"Yeah," Phoebe said quietly. "It's probably the first time I'll ever be good at anything in p.e."

Chris turned and looked at her best friend. Phoebe had barely raised her eyes. Her curly, red hair was falling down into her face, and her motions were slow and uninterested. Even Woody couldn't make her laugh.

She wouldn't talk about what was bothering her, but Chris could guess — Griffin. After falling madly in love with Griffin and breaking up with Brad because of him, Phoebe had not yet accepted it was all over. Griffin had moved to New

York City to be an actor and recently told Phoebe that he didn't want to talk to her anymore. Phoebe had not been herself since the night that Griffin had broken things off.

"What are you going to do over Christmas vacation?" Chris asked Phoebe, trying to get her friend to warm up.

"I don't know yet."

"Maybe we should take some more ski lessons," Sasha volunteered between ravenous bites of her sandwich.

Phoebe put her hand over her eyes and shook her head. As if to end the whole subject, she then reached down under the table and pulled out her book bag. A math book appeared shortly.

Chris traded a look with Sasha. Phoebe just wasn't going to talk. It didn't matter how boisterous, inquisitive, or funny they were, she was keeping her problems with Griffin to herself.

"I'd like to go up to Harwood for the state basketball tournament," Ted said enthusiastically. "But nobody else seems that interested."

"Don't look at me," piped Woody.

"I'm not looking at you, pomegranate breath," retorted Ted, "but Brad might go for it." Ted turned and looked around the crowded, noisy lunchroom. "If I could ever find him to ask him."

Phoebe looked up briefly from her book, let out a huff, and put her head back down.

Suddenly Ted was tugging furiously at Chris's shoulder and pointing the other way across the lunchroom. Woody had stopped counting out his pomegranate seeds, Sasha was putting down her sprouts, and even Phoebe had looked up and was

101

now staring over her math book. Chris turned around, too. There, threading her way through a pack of freshman boys, was Brenda. The look on her face was grim, her movements were hurried, and her destination was clearly their table.

"Brenda, Bren, over here!" Chris waved excitedly and then nudged Ted to make a space and move down. Everybody else at the table seemed to react instantly. Woody picked up his pomegranate seeds, and Sasha her sandwich. Only Phoebe seemed frozen, but it didn't matter — by the time Brenda had arrived there was a space waiting for her to sit down.

"Hi, hi!" Chris said excitedly.

"Hi," Brenda responded in a dead voice.

In that second, Chris felt her hopes drop. Brenda shifted nervously, her arms folded across her stiff denim jacket.

"I just came to ask a question," Brenda said abruptly.

Woody smiled. "Me, too, but then I decided to stay."

Sasha giggled and Ted smiled warmly, but Chris noticed out of the corner of her eye that Phoebe was giving Brenda a hard stare. It was as if the two of them were communicating without words. Whatever they were saying to each other, Chris sensed it wasn't friendly.

"Bren," Chris broke in, "why don't you sit down? It's still a while before class and there's plenty of —"

"That's okay," Brenda said, looking away from Phoebe and holding up one hand. "I just wanted to know if any of you have seen Brad Davidson."

Ted casually drummed the surface of the lunch table with his fingers. "Ol' Davidson is playing again in the student council room. He hardly ever comes out of that place anymore. If you see him, ask him if he wants to go with me to the state tournament."

Brenda nodded seriously and then looked back at Chris. "Thanks for the invitation, but I have to go." She gave one last look to Phoebe, then turned sharply and headed back to the hall.

"Whew!" Woody exclaimed. "What was that all about?"

"It's too bad she wouldn't stay," Sasha commented. "You know, Chris, I really like her."

Chris looked down the table at Phoebe. Her friend's face was once more buried in her math book, and she hadn't said a word.

Brenda ran her hand along the row of blue lockers, touching the top of every handle as she walked nervously down the hall. She'd hated going in the lunchroom and walking over to the crowd's table, but now it was over. She should feel some kind of relief — except there was still Brad to deal with, and Phoebe kept popping up in her mind. The messages she'd gotten from Phoebe back there had been awful. They'd been silent, but they'd said everything. Stay away. Keep out. This is my turf. No matter how open, nice, and friendly Chris and the rest of her friends were, Brenda knew she couldn't sit at that table in a million years.

That was all right. She didn't need that lunchroom scene. She liked eating alone. She had a place near the auditorium, a little niche off the stairwell that led to the balcony where she could take her lunch and read the psychology books that Tony recommended, and figure out how to help the kids at Garfield. That was more important than being part of any crowd or scene, she told herself. The two just didn't go together.

Brenda rounded the corner and stopped. The student council room was supposed to be somewhere nearby. Brenda finally saw a door with a wooden plaque identifying it as "Student Government Association Office." She walked over, paused with her hand on the doorknob, and did a quick grounding exercise. Taking a deep breath and reminding herself that she was doing this for Tony and a lot of kids in real trouble, Brenda opened the door.

Brad was standing at the other end of the room writing dates on the blackboard. He was too preoccupied to notice Brenda when she walked in. His tall figure was stretched to its tallest so that he could reach the very top. His neatly creased pants and red crew neck sweater seemed to be part of an amazingly long and graceful whole.

Brenda inched her way over to a place against the side wall.

"Hello."

Brad stopped writing, brought his arms down, and turned around. There was a flash of recognition and then a big smile. His eyes were big and full of pleased surprise.

"Brenda, hi!" He smiled and walked over to her. He sat down on the back of a desk, his feet resting on the seat. When he looked up at her again, there was a hint of shyness in his face. "Did Chris tell you that I called?" he asked.

Brenda felt her face flush. She didn't know what to say. She reminded herself of her purpose and forged ahead. "Brad, I just came because I wanted to ask you something about the student council."

He looked a little surprised at her curtness. "Sure. What?"

"I have this friend at Garfield House — Tony Martinez — he's the head counselor there." Brad was staring at her. When she met his eye he gave a tentative smile.

"Anyway, Tony is concerned that not enough people are getting the message about Garfield. Kids hit the streets and they don't know where to turn. He wanted me to ask you if he could come to the student council and speak — you know, try and get the word out to everybody that there's a place kids can go who need help."

Brad nodded enthusiastically. "That's exactly what this student council should be doing. How about next week?"

Brenda shifted against the wall. "That would be good."

"Maybe you could get out of class and come, too."

"Maybe." Brenda gave the wall a tiny kick and started to leave. She felt Brad instantly get up from the desk. "That's all I wanted to ask. Thanks."

But Brad slipped in between her and the door before she could open it. "Can I ask *you* something?" he questioned.

105

"What?"

Brad laughed nervously. "Hey, I said yes to your question so you have to say yes to mine."

"What is it?"

Brad's voice came out very softly. "Let's go out to a movie this Saturday night?" He put out his hand and touched the sleeve of her jacket.

Brenda felt herself melt inside. What was it about Brad that made her so ridiculous? He'd deliberately taken advantage of her. Phoebe was his girl friend, so why did Brenda feel like a piece of silly putty?

"I'll pick you up at seven?"

Brenda almost said no. Her insides told her to say it. He was trying to use her again. It was another mean trick. When she looked up, his eyes were still on her.

"Well, I don't know, I —"

"We don't have to go to a movie if you don't want —"

"No, that's okay."

"No, if you'd rather do something else —"

"No, I like movies."

Brad laughed. "This is absurd — again."

Brenda couldn't help smiling. "Yeah," was all she trusted herself to say.

"So, Saturday night at seven." A huge smile revealed Brad's chipped tooth.

Brenda felt as if she were swimming upstream. She couldn't fight it; she was being pushed back down. She would go out with Brad this weekend. "Okay," she whispered, reaching past him for the door.

"Great. See you then."

"Yeah," Brenda answered almost silently, as she rushed back into the hallway.

Brenda walked down the hall without looking back. She wanted to escape that shapeless feeling. She wanted to let Brad know just where they stood with each other. Brenda would go out with Brad, but only for one reason — to let him know exactly what she thought of this whole crummy mess.

Chapter
12

Sasha put a finger on the page in front of her and waved her yogurt spoon with the other hand. "This doesn't work right," she called to no one in particular. Nobody answered back. Sasha sighed — as usual she was alone in the newspaper office working after school.

She was poring over Brenda's essay, trying to figure out how to turn a nine-page composition into two and a half pages. At first, printing the essay had seemed like a great idea, but as she re-read the pages, she began to wish that she had just used some old piece of her own and put Brenda's on the back burner.

"Why is this so long?" she mumbled.

If she cut the beginning, then the end wouldn't make sense, and if she just printed the first half, then she'd have to leave out all the good parts about Tony Martinez. Sasha tossed her empty yogurt container in the trash and reached into her backpack for a bag of trail mix. Maybe that would help her think more clearly.

She closed her eyes and popped a raisin into her mouth. As she chewed she tried to relax, to empty her mind so that inspiration could hit. Sure enough, within a few moments, the perfect idea came to her. She was just starting to mark the pages when she heard a soft knock on the door.

"Just come on in," Sasha called. She smiled broadly when she saw who was there.

"Janie!"

"Hi, Sasha," Janie said in a low voice. "I'm not disturbing you or anything, am I?"

Sasha laughed and got up to escort Janie to her desk. She pulled up a chair, and Janie sat down. "You're not disturbing me," Sasha announced. "It's great to see you. I needed a little disturbing anyway." Janie smiled as Sasha pushed the papers to the other side of her desk.

As she began to speak, Janie nervously tugged at her baggy wool jumper and looked up at Sasha. "I just thought. . . ."

"What, Janie?"

"Well, since I said I'd volunteer for the paper, you know, on the ski trip . . . and my mom thinks it's a good idea and all . . . I just came to see what I should do."

Sasha beamed. "That's fabulous. I didn't want to push you into anything, but there's tons that you can do. Especially right now."

Janie nodded passively.

"Want some?" Sasha offered some of her trail mix to Janie. "No salt."

"No thanks."

Sasha continued to munch. "We really need you. I guess it's flu season or something because everybody's out sick. Maybe you could take over for Alison Forbes until she gets back. Would you be interested in that?"

"What does Alison do?"

"She helps deliver papers to the store owners who place ads. See, we make sure all the stores that buy advertising each get a few copies of the paper the day before it goes out to the whole school. Alison was supposed to deliver the next issue to the stores in the Georgetown neighborhood — that is, before she got sick. It would really help if you could do it instead."

"You mean I just walk around and give them copies of the paper? That's all?"

"Yup. I'll try to find something more interesting for you later on."

"Okay." Janie shrugged.

"You'll do it? Oh, that's great! I have to find the list of stores for you." Sasha picked up her pencil and looked around. "Chuck Couch has been handling the accounts, but he's out sick, too. I guess it's okay if I go through his desk."

Sasha found the list in Chuck's desk drawer and set it before Janie, but a booming voice calling Sasha's name from the hallway prevented further conversation. Both girls turned to see where the explosion of sound came from.

It was John Marquette. He practically filled the doorway. Sasha could tell from his stance that he wasn't there to make her afternoon more pleasant.

"Hiya, foxette," he said, his voice tinged with

110

antagonism. He swaggered into the room, arms folded over his letterman's sweater. He sat on Sasha's desk with his back in Janie's face. "I heard there's a photo of me going in the next issue. I wanted to take a look at it."

Sasha refused to let him intimidate her. "John, I'm talking to Janie right now. Could you please wait a minute?"

Marquette jumped off the desk and stared at Janie with mock surprise. "Sorry," he apologized sarcastically. "I didn't notice Olive Oyl here."

"Her name is Janie. And don't call me a little fox. You're such a male chauvinist."

Marquette backed up and leered at her. "You're even cuter when you get mad." He lumbered over to a stack of photos on a nearby desk and began shuffling through them himself.

Sasha immediately got up. "John, if it's so important to look at a dumb picture of yourself, I'll get it for you. Don't mess up the whole stack."

"Whatever you say, foxette." He stepped back with an exaggerated gesture.

Sasha handed him the photo and sat back down. He examined it with a proud smile.

"Pretty impressive, huh?" He slipped the photo in front of Janie. "What do you think, Olive Oyl?"

"Very nice," Janie managed, turning a shade paler. It was a picture of Marquette in a wrestling leotard pinning down another guy.

Marquette burst out laughing and tossed the photo back onto the pile. "Don't faint, Olive. I didn't hurt him."

"John, you've seen the photo. Now will you please go back to practice?" Sasha demanded.

111

He moved close to her. "I'm going, you little fox. I just wanted to find out one more thing."

"What's that, John?" Sasha was beginning to lose her patience.

He leaned way over the desk. Janie had slid so far down in her chair she was practically on the floor.

"I want to know, foxette, when you're going to do that big front page interview with me."

Sasha rolled her eyes. "John, I told you —"

"See, I was thinking," he interrupted, "my cousin gives this paper a lot of money with those ads he buys every week. Did you ever think what would happen if Superjock stopped running ads in your paper?"

Marquette had a point, and Sasha knew it. Getting advertisers wasn't easy, and Superjock was one of the paper's strongest supporters. *The Red and the Gold* would be in trouble if Superjock pulled out. Still, Marquette's cousin wasn't as big a jerk as John was. He would never pull out his support just because she didn't run a story about his egomaniacal relative.

"Look, John, if I had made some kind of mistake or something with your cousin's ads, then you might have something. But just because he puts an ad in doesn't mean you can tell me what to print."

Marquette thought about that for a moment — a very short moment. He wiped his mouth with the back of his hand. "All right, foxette, all right." He began to back out of the office. "But don't think I'm going to forget about my little fox. 'Cause one day you're going to be begging me for a story. And believe me, that's going to be the day when Marquette gets anything he wants." He laughed dully. "Got it?"

"Yes, John."

Marquette laughed again as he backed toward the door. "Bye, Olive." He blew them both a kiss and strutted out, his choppy laugh filling the empty hallway.

"Aghhh, he makes me so mad," Sasha growled. "He's the only guy who's ever made me wish I was big, really big, so I could let him have it."

But Janie didn't look up. She was too busy reading the list of stores that she would have to visit. Without speaking, she raised her head and pointed to the last name on her list: Superjock Sporting Goods.

Janie's face was full of anxiety. "Will I have to deliver a paper to John Marquette?"

Sasha sighed. "Don't worry. It's just me he's after, because of the paper. Besides, it's all an act. He just does it to prove his masculinity. I'm sure he's really harmless."

Janie tried to smile, but her mouth didn't quite make it.

"Don't let him bother you. He may not even be there when you drop off the paper."

"Okay," Janie said in a shaky voice. "I guess it's better than going back to the radio station."

Sasha smiled sympathetically and ate another raisin.

Chapter
13

"Brenda, what's wrong?"

Brenda and Brad were standing in line only a few feet from the ticket window. They were in the midst of the Saturday night crowd. Brenda didn't want to make a scene. She was waiting for just the right time to tell Brad exactly what she thought of the way he was using her, but she was having difficulty finding it.

"I don't think I really feel like seeing a movie after all."

Brad looked confused and nervous. His tanned forehead was tense, and he kept fastening and unfastening the leather band on his watch.

"Okay," Brad finally said, stepping out of line. "We don't have to go."

Brenda let the people behind her move ahead, while making sure that she didn't stand too close to Brad. She pulled her jacket tight around her body and adjusted the glittery scarf wrapped around her neck.

"Do you want to do something else?" Brad asked anxiously.

"No."

"Well, let's go back to the car, okay?"

Brenda didn't answer. She put her fists in her pockets and started walking. She wondered when she was going to tell him, when she was going to deliver her speech. It was proving harder than she'd expected.

They walked away from the theater. Brenda could almost feel the silence pressing in on her. Brad was walking slowly, as if he wanted to give her time to change her mind. Maybe he thought it would turn into the situation at Mount Jackson: She would run off and he could catch her and everything would be just fine.

When they reached the car, Brad stopped before opening the door. "Look," he said quietly, "what's going on? If you don't want to go out with me, or if you'd rather be with somebody else, please tell me. I don't know if you're playing some kind of game."

"It's not a game," Brenda shot back.

Brad looked at her. There was hurt in his eyes that she hadn't expected, and she had a fleeting moment of doubt. But she reminded herself that he was using her; all the events of the previous weekend demonstrated it.

"If you don't want to tell me what's going on, let's just forget the whole thing and I'll take you home," Brad finally said.

This was it. She had rehearsed the words so many times. Now it was real, and she hoped she got it right.

"I want to tell you something, and then I want you to take me home," she began. "I know what's going on here. I know that the only reason you're paying attention to me is to make Phoebe jealous."

"What?" Brad looked shocked.

Brenda ignored his reaction and plowed ahead. "I knew it at Mount Jackson and I know it now. And I think it's really low." She couldn't finish. There was an unexpected tug at the back of her throat.

"How could you think that?"

Brenda angrily swept a layer of hair away from her face. She had pinned it up, but half of it was already falling down. Drawing a deep breath, she made herself go on. "It's so obvious. The first time you asked me to ski with you was only because Phoebe was watching and I —"

"Wait a minute," Brad answered, clearly upset. Brenda started to take a step away, but he blocked her path.

"Maybe that's a little bit true," Brad admitted. "When I first asked if you wanted to ski, I guess it was because I wanted to make Phoebe jealous, but not after that."

"Come on," Brenda protested.

"No, not after that," Brad insisted. "I don't know where you got that idea, but it's really wrong! After you took that fall and we talked, and on the way home, couldn't you tell how I really felt?"

Now it was Brenda who was confused. Brad's

voice, the determined look in his eyes, all told her that he was sincere. It was possible that she had misjudged the situation. She had certainly done it before. The possibility that she had made such a terrible mistake with someone she really cared for threw her head into a whirlwind. For one girl, she managed to do a huge number of dumb things.

Brad stuck his hands in his pockets and walked away from the car toward the edge of the lot. He picked up an empty soda can from the asphalt and pitched it over the chain link fence that separated the parking lot from the construction site next to it. "I don't believe this," he muttered.

Brenda followed without thinking. What had she done now? Her head was starting to ache. "Brad, I —"

He angrily turned back to her. "Do you have any idea how hard it was for me to ask you out? It's true that I've been really hung up on Phoebe for a long time, but this is the first time I really feel like I'm over her, and that's because of you. Now you tell me I just want to make Phoebe jealous. This has nothing to do with her."

Brad went all the way up to the fence and laced his hands in the wire. His back to Brenda, he stared off at a half-built structure on the other side.

A strong wind blew across the open lot, and Brenda wrapped her arms around herself. Under her jean jacket she was only wearing a lacy T-shirt and skirt, and the cold cut through her. She had ruined everything once again. She walked slowly over to the fence and stood next to Brad. For a fleeting moment she thought that it would

117

be simpler to climb over that fence and run away. But she didn't want to do that this time. This time she would face the mess she'd made.

"I'm sorry. I guess I was wrong," she admitted. "I was just afraid of being made a fool of."

Brad threw back his head and laughed. It was a sad, ironic laugh. "This is so ridiculous. I don't know who's more paranoid, you or me."

"What do you mean?"

Brad gave the fence a slight shake. "I had already decided that you were acting weird because you really wanted to be with some other guy instead of me. I never thought it was the other way around."

Now it was Brenda who was shocked. "Why would you think I wanted to be with someone else?"

Brad shrugged. "Why would you think I would just use you to make Phoebe jealous?"

"I've had people treat me pretty weirdly in the past."

"And I had a girl suddenly dump me for somebody else in the past, too."

Brenda put her hand on Brad's arm. She was beginning to realize that in his own way, he was just as frightened as she was. Brad pulled away. He let go of the fence and began walking slowly to his car. He leaned against the hood. Brenda walked over closer to him.

"I'm sorry," Brad said softly. "I was really looking forward to tonight."

"I'm sorry, too."

"This whole thing is one dumb mess. I just want to get to know you and start again, not keep

118

being hung up on what happened with Phoebe."

"It's my fault."

"No." Brad looked toward the street, his face drawn and tired. "Do you still want me to take you home?"

Brenda looked steadily at him. She suddenly wanted to reach out and hold him, let him know how she really felt. But she couldn't find the nerve. "No. I don't want to go home," she said simply. Brad met her eye and she offered a thin smile. "I do want you to tell me what happened with you and Phoebe. Maybe then we can get rid of the whole thing."

A car drove by and its headlights passed over Brad's face. Brenda could see his hesitation, but he looked at her again and seemed to find new courage. Still leaning back against the car, he reached for her hand. He stared at her palm as if he was trying to read her fortune. "There's not all that much to tell. Phoebe and I had been together for two years and I thought everything was fine. I went away to Princeton to have an interview for college next year and when I came back a day later Phoebe told me she was in love with somebody else."

"You mean out of nowhere?"

Brad nodded. "Yeah. I had no idea she was even seeing this guy. Griffin Neill is his name. He left school to go to New York to be an actor after that. But the worst thing was that I felt like such a fool — and the jealousy. I was so mad I didn't know what to do."

"I know how that is."

"Yeah. And for the last two months I've been a

119

total basket case. Anyway, it's all over now." He smiled sadly and cupped both of his hands over hers. A surge of warmth shot through her.

"I'm beginning to think the break-up was a really good thing. I think I used to take a lot of things for granted. You know, I'm so busy with stuff at school that I have a tendency to forget about everything else. I also learned that it's important to talk about things, find out what's going on in the other person's head. That's what I liked so much about you. You seemed to talk about stuff that really mattered to you, after we got through the beginning weirdness. I just felt as if you were somebody who was really in touch with what was important."

"Me?" Brenda laughed. "Are you kidding? I'm usually so busy running away from everything that I don't even know what's going on."

Brad let go of her hands and encircled her waist with his arms. He pulled her gently to him. "I know about last year. But look what you're doing at the halfway house now. That's a lot more important than leading a bunch of meetings at school. You're really helping people deal with the hardest kinds of problems."

Brad was looking at her with such loving eyes that after a moment Brenda had to look away. Something new and scary was happening to her. Her breath started to quicken and her stomach did a slow skydive. She felt his hand gently push a few strands of hair away from her mouth, and she had to close her eyes. Her head fell onto Brad's shoulder and she buried herself in his clean, warm smell.

"Hey." He touched the back of her hair. "I think we missed the beginning of the movie." He laughed softly. "I have to admit, I didn't get the feeling you were real excited about seeing it."

Brenda smiled and leaned in until the length of her whole body was against his. Brad's arms pulled her in harder and she clasped her hands around his waist. For a moment they simply held each other, with urgency and care.

Brad relaxed his arms and Brenda stepped back. "Maybe we should just start this whole evening over." He smiled coyly and held out his hand to shake. "Hi."

Brenda started to laugh and shook his hand. "Hi."

"Do you usually hang out in parking lots on Saturday night?"

Brenda laughed. "Well, I did have a date, but I acted like such a jerk that he left me here."

"Sounds like the guy was kind of a jerk, too."

"One jerk deserves another." They both smiled.

Brad walked around and opened the car door. "Maybe I can steal you away from this jerk." He bowed cornily and waved her into the car. "What do you say? I don't promise to be much better than the guy who left you here, but you could give me a chance."

Brenda took a deep, cold breath. She was suddenly so light and giddy that she was almost dizzy. "I guess I'll take the risk." She climbed back into the car. A second later Brad slipped into the driver's seat.

He looked over at her and ran his fingertips lightly across her cheek. "You know what? I think we should make this date different from the very start."

"You do?"

"I sure do." Brad leaned toward her. He had a dreamy expression as he slid his hand around the back of her neck. He slowly kissed her, first her nose, then her cheeks, her chin, her forehead. He ended at her mouth. Brenda felt she might melt into nothing, but she didn't try to escape the feeling.

Brad relaxed his arms and smiled at her. "Take two, Brenda and Brad. I think we'll get it right this time."

Chapter
14

The newspaper was hot off the press. That's what Janie thought people said — "hot off the press." Of course, her copies of *The Red and the Gold* weren't really hot and there was no printing press at Kennedy High. But Sasha had stopped by the Rose Hill printer Tuesday afternoon and brought a stack to Janie. After school that day, Janie tucked her twenty copies under her arm and took the bus to Georgetown to deliver them.

There were only four stores Janie had to visit. A Roy Rogers fast-food restaurant, an exercise studio called The Body Store, the Rezato clothing boutique, and Superjock sporting goods. Janie thought she'd visit them in that order. That way if she was lucky, and there was a snowstorm in the next hour, she would have an excuse to avoid the last one. Janie stared out the window of the bus and fantasized she would be tied up and held hostage in the kitchen of the Roy Rogers. She would save the lives of women, children, and a couple of men and no one would care that she had never made it to see John Marquette at Superjock. Janie was just getting to the part in her daydream where she was interviewed on the news when she realized that the bus was almost at the Roy Rogers. She pulled the cord just in time to make her stop.

With her newspapers under her arm, Janie hurried down the block and into the fast-food restaurant. She wasn't sure who to hand the papers to, however, so she stood at the end of the order line.

"What would you like?" said the girl when Janie finally arrived at the counter.

"Um. I guess nothing. I'm supposed to give you a copy of the Kennedy High paper. You have an ad in it." Janie opened the paper and showed the advertisement to the countergirl.

The girl's expression changed from boredom to delight. She took the paper. "Rhonda, look at this ad! Isn't it good?" She held up the paper and pointed the full page ad at Rhonda, the manager. Janie had to admit it was an impressive ad. The logo was surrounded with charming Christmas cartoons and the sheer size made it impossible to ignore. Rhonda came rushing over.

"How marvelous," Rhonda exclaimed happily. "I had no idea our ad would be so big! I thought I ordered a small one, but this is marvelous! Who brought this? You?" Janie nodded. "Oh, it's wonderful!"

"Can I have one for myself?" the countergirl asked. Janie gladly gave a copy to her.

"How about me?" called a high voice from behind the french fries. Janie passed another copy back.

"Thank you," glowed Rhonda. "You tell your school they did a marvelous job! This is the first time we bought an ad and I'm just tickled. What's your name?"

"Janie Barstow."

"Well, Janie, this is marvelous! How about a complimentary burger and fries?"

"Gee, okay," Janie answered. Maybe this wasn't such a bad job after all. Janie couldn't remember the last time she was the center of such attention. She gratefully accepted her free food and sat down to eat. The whole time Rhonda smiled at her.

"Would you like a few more copies?" Janie asked as she finished her hamburger.

"If I could. Oh, that would be marvelous!"

Janie carefully saved three copies for her next three stops and left the rest of the papers on the order counter.

"Thank you." Rhonda waved at Janie as she walked toward the door.

"Bye," Janie replied brightly. Feeling refreshed and confident, Janie tossed her book bag over her shoulder and went back outside.

It was sunny and cold and the street was crisscrossed with red and green garlands. Janie was beginning to think that maybe she would stay on the newspaper, even after Alison came back.

Maybe she could help with the layout or organizing the ads. She knew she would be good at that. With a new purpose in her step, Janie found the address of The Body Shop and went in.

The woman behind the counter wore a perfectly coordinated exercise outfit and thanked Janie for the paper without looking inside. Janie was about to remind the woman to check the ad, but she ran off shouting that she knew it was fine and thanks to Janie again for taking the trouble to drop it off and to continue her ad the same as before. She gave Janie a big smile and a wave before disappearing down a carpeted hall. A second later a loud rock beat filled the foyer and Janie could just see down to a mirrored room full of women bending over at the waist and bouncing their torsos up and down.

Janie smiled to herself as she looked up the destination of her next delivery. Rezata boutique was all the way at the other end of Georgetown, but Janie was feeling so good she decided to take her time and walk. Window-shopping all the way, she enjoyed the decorations and the crowds, barely noticing that it was almost dark by the time she reached the boutique.

The chicest clothing store in Georgetown, Rezato was not a place Janie usually went into. She glanced at the window display (a snowman in a bikini surrounded by multicolored sweaters), buttoned up her coat to hide her wrinkled wool jumper, and went in.

The store was empty except for an older woman behind the counter who was examining an account book. Janie walked up and took out one of her two remaining copies of *The Red and the Gold*. She stared at the dark roots of the woman's reddish hair and waited.

"Yes?" the woman said finally, her voice very nasal. She gave Janie a quick, practiced smile.

"Hi. Is the manager here?"

"I'm the manager." The woman puffed up the sides of her hair with her pencil.

Janie opened the paper to the Rezato ad. The artwork had been done by a Kennedy student and Janie knew the woman would be impressed. Carefully, Janie turned the page to give the manager the most advantageous view.

"This is your ad in *The Red and the Gold*." Janie pointed to the quarter-page drawing. "I think it's the best one in the whole issue," she added with a touch of pride.

The woman almost smiled as she slipped on a pair of bifocals. When she saw the ad more clearly her face showed real pleasure — for about one second. Then her satisfied expression crumbled and her mouth tightened. She pushed the newspaper away and began to riffle through her account book.

"Wait a minute," she warned, her voice even harsher than before. She was skimming over a list of figures with a long fingernail. "I thought so." She tore off her glasses.

"What is it?" Janie asked, her shyness instantly returning.

The woman pointed to her book with the edge of her glasses. "What does that say?"

Slightly panicked, Janie tried to read the messy script, but she couldn't make any sense out of it. "I —"

The woman whipped the book back around. "It says, dear, full-page ad. Do you see that? Full-page ad!"

Janie glanced at the ledger again and was able to make out those words.

"What do you call that?" The woman pointed to the newspaper.

"I guess that's only a quarter of a page, isn't it?"

The manager shook her head in disgust. "It certainly is. I should have known you high school kids couldn't handle something like this. Dear, it's Christmas, the busiest season of the year. What good is a little ad like that going to do me? And besides that, we paid for a full-page!"

Janie wished she could crawl quietly into one of the dressing rooms. "I'm sorry. I'll tell them about the mistake. I'm sure they'll give you a credit for next time or something like that."

"At the very least," the woman said nastily.

"I'll tell them at school tomorrow. I don't know what else to say."

The woman let out a disgusted huff. She circled the ad with her pencil. "Give me another copy of this. I'm going to have to send one to the owner."

Janie looked down in a panic. She only had one copy left and she had to deliver that to Superjock.

"They only printed a small batch today. I have one left, but I have to give it to another store. I can get you as many copies as you want to-morrow."

"Dear," the woman insisted, "this is your mistake. I need another copy for the owner!"

Janie's stomach was hurting. She just wanted to go home and crawl into her basement and read. "Here." Janie handed the woman her last newspaper. "Sorry about the problem."

The first thing Janie saw when she stepped outside was Superjock Sporting Goods. The store was directly across the street. Janie even thought she saw John Marquette standing behind the front window. What was she going to do? She shouldn't have given so many copies to the Roy Rogers, but it was too late now to go all the way back and get one. She was just going to have to explain and hope that Marquette didn't humiliate her.

Janie put her head down and slowly entered the athletic shop. Fortunately, Marquette had disappeared, and lots of customers milled through the store. A young man with a strong build immediately came up to her.

"Can I help you?"

Janie made her move. "Yes. I'm from *The Red and the Gold* newspaper staff and —"

"Oh, you probably want to talk to John. He just went into the stockroom, but I'll go and —"

Janie almost put her hand over the young man's mouth.

"No," she said quickly, backing up as she talked. "Just tell him that the newspapers from *The Red and the Gold* were delayed and he won't get his copy until tomorrow."

"Oh, no. He's been waiting for it. There's a photo of him in this issue. Maybe you'd better tell him yourself."

"That's okay," Janie said, almost out the door. "Tell him sorry, he'll get it tomorrow."

The salesman said something else, but Janie was already halfway down the block.

Chapter
15

"Is that Brenda?"

Sasha Jenkins peered sideways around the locker door and blinked her eyes. She and Chris huddled back against the wall of lockers, trying to hide behind the open door.

"Doesn't she look great?" Chris whispered. They both stuck their heads out again like two spies and caught another glimpse. This time they saw Brad run up to Brenda and give her a tiny kiss.

"Did you see that?" Sasha squealed, trying to keep her voice down. Chris clapped her hand over Sasha's mouth and they both started to giggle. "It's so romantic." Sasha leaned back against the locker in a mock faint. "I wish somebody felt that way about me." She giggled again and fanned herself with her math homework.

"Since they went out over the weekend, Brenda

has been on cloud nine. And look at him, Sash. When did you last see Brad that happy?"

Both girls peered around the edge of the locker door once more and stared.

Brenda and Brad were standing close to each other, both animated and bright. They smiled, looked down — but only for a second before being drawn back together again. They somehow managed to be aware only of each other in the midst of the chaos between classes. Brenda was wearing clothes that Chris had seen on her a hundred times before: jeans, a long sweater vest over a lacy T-shirt, and a scarf. Her hair lay against her back in the same uneven waves, but she looked completely different. Gone was the hostile posturing, the sullen look, and angry scowl that had made her lovely face look so hard and tough.

"Did you tell her what we did?" Sasha whispered.

Chris checked to make sure she couldn't be seen and leaned back against the lockers. "No. I thought it would be better not to. If I hadn't tricked her into the ski trip, she wouldn't have said yes to that."

"Are you sure it will be okay?" Sasha bit her lower lip.

"Look what happened from the ski trip." Chris pointed to Brad.

"All right. I'm going to tell her about it in Barnes's class, next period. I have to rush to the newspaper office before class." Sasha started to leave, but Chris put a hand on her arm and leaned over with sudden urgency.

"Sash, have you seen Phoebe today?"

Sasha frowned. "No, but yesterday she was so bummed out she was barely talking."

Chris nervously rolled a piece of blond hair around her finger. "I'm a little worried. I ask her what's wrong and she keeps telling me it's nothing."

"The whole thing with Griffin was a pretty big blow. Give her time."

"I guess. Let's look for her at lunch today. Yesterday I think she stayed in the choir room."

"Good idea. Look, I've got to run if I'm going to make it to the newspaper office before Barnes's class." Sasha started to go. Brenda and Brad were just disappearing down the other end of the hall, their arms wound around each other's waists. "Look at those two. I wish I had a sister who was as good a matchmaker as you are."

Chris grinned. "I just set the wheels in motion. They did the rest."

Chris and Sasha traded excited smiles and rushed off in opposite directions.

"I think everybody's getting tired of staring at us," Brenda joked as Brad was walking her to Barnes's English class.

"You disappointed?" He laughed. "Everyone just wants to check out who's with who, and then forget about it. I don't care."

"I know you don't." Brenda entwined her fingers with Brad's.

"Will you meet me right at the beginning of lunch so we can wait for this Tony Martinez guy?"

Brenda nodded. Tony was visiting the student council during fifth period. She had volunteered to help Brad set up and to introduce them.

"I can only stay for the first ten minutes of the meeting, though."

"Why?"

"That's all Turnbell would let me out of fifth period for. Math is not exactly my strongest subject."

"Okay. I wish you could stay for the whole thing, but if Turnbell wants to be a creep, what can we do?" Brad brushed a stray hair away from her forehead. "I'll just grab some lunch and meet you as soon as I can outside the council room. Does Tony know where to find us?"

"I told him."

Brad backed off, heading in the other direction. "I'll be there five minutes after lunch starts," he called, still backing up. A freshman picked just that moment to cut across the hall and Brad almost crashed into him. Both boys apologized, then Brad turned back to Brenda with a silly, embarrassed shrug. "Bye," he yelled happily.

Brenda giggled and waved. "Bye."

Brad was now running and calling over his shoulder, "See you then."

"Okay." Brenda laughed.

He kept running, but turned back once more to jump up and wave, this time almost smacking into the twelfth-grade vice-principal, who picked just that moment to walk by. Mr. Cilento glared disapprovingly at Brad and marched off. Brad laughed, held his hand over his mouth in mock horror, and waved again. Brenda watched him until he was completely out of sight.

Unable to hide her giddiness, Brenda went into English class and sat down. She had been feeling so light the last few days that every once in a while she took hold of something solid just to make sure she didn't float away. She knew it was silly, but as she sat down at her desk she grabbed the sides hard. She had never felt quite like this before.

When Brenda saw the big brown folder on the top of Barnes's desk, her spirits had to sink a little. The large legal folder was stuffed full of papers and that meant only one thing. Barnes had graded their essays and would be returning them that period.

Brenda made herself stay calm. She was even more secure than before about her essay. She was starting to believe that everything she touched didn't have to turn into a mess. She was even realizing that she could make mistakes and figure out how to fix them. Part of her new confidence came from Brad and the faith he had in her, but part of it came from inside herself.

A few seconds after the bell rang, Sasha rushed in, her arms full of books and newspapers. She gave Mr. Barnes an apologetic look, wiped a few beads of sweat off her flushed forehead, and sat down across from Brenda. Offering Brenda a thrilled smile, she quickly calmed down when Barnes called the class to order.

"Nice of you to make it, Sasha," Mr. Barnes began drolly. He took roll, tapping his pencil once for each student. When he finished, he boosted himself onto the edge of his desk and hiked up the perfect crease in his slacks. Hands folded, he addressed the class.

"Everybody in a good mood today?" Mr. Barnes asked loudly. There were a few snickers. Jim Edmundson said he wasn't going to be as soon as they got their papers back. Nobody laughed.

"Well, I hope you're all in a good mood, because I do have your essays today. Overall, we didn't do badly."

Brenda swallowed hard.

After pulling the papers out of the portfolio, Mr. Barnes smiled, and came right toward Brenda. It always happened this way. Austin came first.

"Brenda," Mr. Barnes began, stretching out to hand her the essay. But he stopped and turned to look at the rest of the class. Brenda reached for her paper, but Barnes was waving it in the air. "Let me say one thing," he offered.

Brenda held her breath.

"This was by far the best paper I've ever had from you and by far the best one turned in. Now that I know you can do this kind of work, I'm not settling for anything less."

With that, Mr. Barnes winked at Brenda and dropped the essay onto her desk. Immediately she saw the grade at the top of the paper: *A — Very well done! Let's see more of this!*

Sasha was leaning over to look at the grade on Brenda's paper.

"I knew it," Sasha whispered. "I knew it was right!"

Brenda was still staring at the neat red letters at the top of her paper. The essay was something she had done by herself, that reflected what was really taking place within her, and Barnes had said it was good — more than good. He said it was "very well done," which in anybody else's terms meant terrific. And terrific was just how Brenda felt.

Mr. Barnes walked to the back of the class and continued slowly to hand back papers, stopping occasionally to give extra comments. While he was occupied with Marty Steele, Sasha leaned way over and tapped Brenda on the arm.

"Your essay was so good," Sasha whispered.

"What?"

Brenda was confused by Sasha's comment and wrinkled her nose. Sasha pointed her pen to a piece of paper, indicating that she would write Brenda a note, and ripped out a sheet of paper.

Sasha wrote furiously, not even looking up to check the grade on her own essay. A few moments later she pulled the new issue of the school newspaper out of her backpack and slid it onto Brenda's lap. Then Sasha handed over her note. Brenda opened it and discreetly began to read.

Brenda,

I wish I could tell you out loud, but Barnes would kill me and I can't stand to wait until the end of the period. I am so excited! The copy of *The Red and the Gold* is the new issue. Just came out, will be circulated today at lunch. Open it to page 2 and then come back to this note.

At that point in the note, elaborately drawn arrows pointed to the newspaper. Sasha was watching Brenda intently. When Brenda gave her a curious look, Sasha gestured to the paper and smiled with anticipation.

Baffled, Brenda opened *The Red and the Gold* to page 2 and scanned it. Then she saw it, just at the top of the second page. Her own name — Brenda Austin. Next she saw the title of her essay: "Making a Difference." Last she saw her own words in dark newsprint. She dropped the paper on her desk and put both her hands over mouth to quell her shock and horror. Her essay about Tony Martinez and Garfield was printed in the Kennedy newspaper for everyone to read.

In a panic, Brenda read the second part of Sasha's note.

Part 2: I'm sorry I had to cut your essay, but there was only so much space on the page and we really wanted to make sure it got in. That guy Tony seems really amazing, so I tried to keep in all the parts about him at least. I think it's a great piece of writing. So did Chris! That's why she gave it to me. CONGRATULATIONS!!!

Brenda dropped the note onto the top of her desk. Chris! Chris! Chris had given her essay to the newspaper. How could she do something like that?

Her heart pounding, Brenda lowered her head to read her own article. By the time she finished, her blood was pumping even faster and her hands were like ice.

The way that her article had been cut for the paper it was no longer about Garfield House and the kids. It was now more of a profile of Tony. So much so that it took on a whole new meaning. Read in a certain way, the essay almost implied that Brenda was in love with Tony — that he was the most important person in her life! Brenda prayed that everyone wouldn't read it that way.

But Brenda didn't really care about everyone. There was only one person who would be hurt if he interpreted her article the wrong way. And Brad was the person Brenda really was thinking about.

Chapter
16

Brad carefully dialed the combination on his lock as he stood in the middle of the locker room aisle. His hair was still wet, and a towel was loosely wrapped around his waist, but he was in a hurry. As soon as the bell rang he'd race out, grab some lunch, and get back to the student council room to meet Brenda. He wanted everything to be just right for her friend from the halfway house. His presentation might turn out to launch a really important project at Kennedy.

"Hey, look here," a low voice crowed from the other end of a row of lockers. "Hey, lookee at the numero uno, all-around athlete, and Mr. Studly. Hey, Stark, what do you think of my picture?"

Brad glanced up and saw John Marquette holding up a copy of the school newspaper, and cramming it into classmate Michael Stark's face.

"Get lost, Marquette," Stark said bravely. "That's the ugliest picture I've ever seen."

Brad went back to his locker combination. Marquette was one of the biggest jerks at Kennedy High. He was also an incredible athlete and stronger than anybody in the senior class. Poor Stark was about half Marquette's size, but at least he was feisty. He wasn't letting Marquette push him around.

"What's wrong?" Marquette boomed. "You don't like my picture? Hey, maybe you'd like it better if I took you outside and hung you from one of the basketball hoops."

Brad opened his locker door and grabbed his T-shirt. He glanced down the row and saw that Stark had backed up against the row of lockers facing Marquette straight on. "I told you," Stark yelled, "I don't want to look at it. Now get lost."

Marquette reached out at Stark and grabbed him by his shirt collar, pushing him against his locker. Stark winced and struggled, but his size made it a pitiful match. Brad couldn't just stand there. He slipped his pants on and walked over to where Marquette had Stark pinned.

"John, cool it."

"Hey, Brad baby," Marquette said in a snide voice. "Stark over here doesn't want to look at my picture."

Brad shook his head. Marquette was egomania defined. He couldn't believe that everybody wasn't just hanging on his latest athletic accomplishment.

"Let him go, John."

Marquette looked over his shoulder at Brad, his big beefy face wrapped in a sneer. "What's wrong, Mr. Student Body President? Afraid somebody's going to get hurt?"

Brad planted his feet as the locker room suddenly got quiet. People were used to Marquette's tirades. Usually they didn't go very far before a teacher called him on it, but right now Mr. Mattson was still in the gym. Brad wasn't nearly so broad as Marquette, but he was almost as tall. If there was going to be a fight, it would be one to remember.

"You want somebody to look at your picture, I'll look," Brad said coolly. "Now let go of Michael."

"Yeah, let go of me, sausage head," Stark shouted.

Marquette loosened his grip on Stark and turned all the way around. He faced Brad squarely and brought the copy of *The Red and the Gold* into his face.

"Okay," he said nastily. "You can look at my picture, then. In fact, you can look at more than my picture. You seen the article by your new little girl friend yet?"

Brad flinched. Marquette was really starting to get to him. It would be dumb to get into a fight in the locker room — it could even go down on his record — but if the jerk was going to try to bring Brenda into it, he had no choice.

"Here, look." Marquette thrust the paper in Brad's face. To his amazement, Brad saw an article just above the wrestler's photo that had Brenda's name attached to it. He grabbed the paper out of Marquette's hand.

"Ah ha," Marquette roared, looking around the locker room at everybody else. "See, now he believes me. Davidson's new fox writes an article about some other guy and doesn't bother to tell him about it herself."

Marquette looked back at Brad, who was now scanning the article. "Looks like your fox has quite a reputation with other guys from what her article says," he jabbed.

Now the locker room fell silent. Michael Stark shut his locker slowly and slipped a few feet away. Brad kept reading, trying to understand the words on the page. It was by Brenda all right, but it didn't make any sense. It was an article about Tony — the guy she knew at the halfway house — only it sounded like —

"From what I see in the paper, sounds like your new girl friend is the type to dump you just like your old girl friend," Marquette explained for the benefit of everybody in the locker room. "Sounds like she's got the hots for some other guy already. Poor old student body president gets dumped again."

Brad looked up slowly. He wasn't aware of the paper now, wasn't even aware of the twenty-five other guys staring at him. All he could see was Marquette's big, beefy face just a few feet in front of him. His hand curled up in a fist.

"Go ahead, Braddy waddy," Marquette taunted. "Go ahead and take the first swing."

Brad lunged toward the athlete, bringing his fist up to meet Marquette's chin, when he felt a powerful hand wrenching his arm to a halt.

"That's enough, Davidson!" Mr. Mattson called out.

Brad immediately dropped his arm, although he continued to scowl at Marquette. "What's going on here?" he demanded.

"Nothing," Brad said quietly.

Mr. Mattson frowned. "What do you mean nothing? Marquette, what happened?"

"Oh, Davidson here just got a little hot under the collar over this article his girl friend wrote for the paper and I guess I got in his way. You saw him, he was about to take a swing at me."

Mr. Mattson didn't look any more satisfied with Marquette's explanation, but it was obvious he wasn't going to get to the bottom of the disagreement.

"Listen you two, no fighting or I'm going to knock both of your heads together. Got that?"

"I got it," Marquette said quickly, beginning to pick up his notebook and look for an exit.

"What about you, Davidson?"

Brad still couldn't take his eyes from Marquette's ugly face. His fist was aching to make a connection with that thick skull. But Brad was also slightly stunned. What did that article in *The Red and the Gold* mean? Brenda hadn't told him anything about it.

"Did you hear what I said, Davidson?" Mr. Mattson added loudly.

"Yes, sir."

"All right, all of you, dress and get out of here."

Brad went back to his locker as Marquette made a swift exit. Michael Stark came over and laid a hand on Brad's shoulder. "Thanks, guy," he offered.

144

Brad shrugged. "It's okay. I just wish the big ape would pick on somebody his own size."

"He's too much of a coward for that," Stark reasoned. "He only wanted you to take a swing at him because he knew Mattson had just walked into the locker room. He knows you've got the best academic record in the class and he can't stand anybody having anything he can't."

Brad nodded. He no longer cared about John Marquette. He slipped his shirt on, hastily tucking it in, then pulled on his socks and shoes and grabbed his sweater. He was late. Brenda would be waiting. He slammed his locker door and bent to tie his shoes.

"Anyway, thanks again Brad," Michael offered. "And I know it isn't true about your girl friend."

Brad suddenly whirled around. "What?" he demanded angrily.

Stark looked surprised. He rubbed his hands together and shook his head.

"I just mean that dumb garbage Marquette was saying about Brenda. Everybody knows he's just trying to get to you."

Brad sighed and reached out to shake Michael's hand.

"Thanks. I needed to hear that. Frankly, I'm glad you stood up to the ox. He's such a jerk."

"Well, thanks again."

"That's okay."

Michael left and Brad looked down and saw the now crumpled copy of *The Red and the Gold* lying a few feet away on the floor. He picked up his books and grabbed the paper. Marquette's photo was plastered all over the page, but more important was Brenda's article. He couldn't understand it. What could it possibly mean and why hadn't Brenda told him about it before?

Brad walked out of the locker room with his head bent over the crumpled pages, still tucking in his shirt, but taking in every word.

Chapter
17

Brenda pushed her way through the Kennedy hallway. She had to get to the council room and find Brad before someone told him about her article, or he stumbled across it himself.

She squeezed between two football players and pushed open the double doors to the stairwell, then flew down the stairs. Turning right, she craned her neck and looked through the hordes of people passing by the student council room. No Brad.

She waited. The crowd began to thin. Soon there were only stragglers who had stayed after class or couples rushing off, trying to avoid Mr. Armand, the hall monitor. Ten minutes went by and still Brad hadn't shown. Brenda sat on the single step and put her head down, pressing her knees against her cheeks. She stayed that way, taking deep, wavering breaths until she heard his voice and saw him walking deliberately toward her. Brenda got up to meet him.

"Hi," Brad said. He was standing before her in a pressed blue shirt and navy cords. His face was drawn, his mouth tight, and from the look in his eyes, Brenda knew that the damage had already been done.

"Hi," Brenda answered tentatively.

"It took me longer than I thought," Brad began formally, "because I had to stop and read this." He pulled the newspaper from behind his back and held it out to Brenda. It seemed to dangle there in his hands like it was something contaminated.

"Brad, I'm as upset about it as you are."

"I thought you didn't like to play games," Brad countered angrily, folding the newspaper.

Brenda tried to steady herself. She had to make clear to Brad exactly what the situation was. It would be easier to turn around angrily and walk off. But if she did, the misunderstanding would only get worse, perhaps become irreparable.

"My essay was much longer to begin with," Brenda said quietly. "Sasha cut it so it sounded like I have some kind of thing going with Tony. It's not like that at all. Besides, I didn't even know it was being printed."

Brad looked unconvinced. Brenda could see there was pain in his face, mixed with real anger. He had jammed his fists into his pockets, and he was tracing a pattern over the linoleum with his loafer.

"Brenda," he said, looking at her, nervously adjusting his collar. "I don't know what to think.

148

I want to believe that this article doesn't mean anything."

"It doesn't," Brenda added hastily. "There is nothing between me and Tony. There never has been."

Brad still looked skeptical. He looked over his shoulder and kicked once at the floor. Brenda recognized the emotional tug-of-war going on inside him. She was familiar with all the signs.

A hoot from the other end of the hallway broke the uneasy silence and Brenda looked over. Before she could react, Tony Martinez was rushing towards her, his brawny arms open wide, his face filled with affection.

"Brenda! How's my favorite girl?" Tony shouted gleefully as he picked Brenda up and swung her around in a playful hug.

Brenda went limp. She felt like Tony might as well keep swinging and toss her over a cliff — it couldn't have been much worse. As Tony swung her around, she caught a glimpse of Brad. His features were frozen, and Brenda would have given anything to put her arm out and reassure him. But there was absolutely nothing she could do. Tony finally let her down, still keeping his arm protectively around her shoulder.

Brad stared at them both. Moisture shone in his eyes, and he furiously brushed it away with his cuff.

Tony stuck out a muscular forearm. "I'm Tony Martinez." He grinned.

"I know," Brad answered coldly. Without shaking Tony's outstretched hand, he quickly turned and went into the classroom.

Brenda felt something snap inside. She really did want to run — get away from Kennedy — to be anywhere else.

"What's wrong?" Tony asked.

Brenda looked up at him. She remembered all the times she had run to him. If she had learned anything from Tony's guidance, it was that she eventually had to stop running. Brenda ground her heel into the floor. She would stay put this time, somehow face Brad and tell the truth.

"Don't worry, Tony, I can figure it out," Brenda heard herself say.

Tony smiled and gave Brenda a little hug. He let go as the first batch of student council members arrived.

"Can you stay and answer questions?" Tony asked.

Brenda shook her head. "I can only stay for the first ten minutes. After that I have to go back to math class. So I won't be able to see you afterward." Brenda stepped aside as more council members filed into the classroom. She looked in through the wire-mesh window of the door and saw that the room was already half full. There was no way she could explain the truth to Brad now. She would have to wait until after school.

Tony gently guided her towards the door. "Whatever it is, I'm sure you can handle it." He smiled. "I have faith in you."

Brenda tried to smile back and followed Tony into the room.

In seventh period p.e., Brenda swam laps in the indoor pool. With every stroke, she blew out a frustrated breath, then slapped the water again. She was swimming so furiously her arms ached and she wondered if she was splashing water half-way across the pool.

Brenda jarred her wrist at the edge of the pool and started to make her turn. She felt a hand on her arm and saw Miss Kahn, her gym teacher, crouching over her. As Brenda lifted her head out of the water, she heard the tag end of her name.

"Austin!" Miss Kahn was yelling.

Brenda turned back the flaps of her bathing cap. "Yes?"

"That's enough. Trying to set a new world record? Go on, into the showers."

Brenda nodded and pulled herself out of the water. It was cold and the concrete around the pool was rough and slippery — Brenda's eyes were smarting. She grabbed her towel and took quick, careful steps to the dressing room.

Rinsing the residue of chlorine off her body, Brenda made a decision. She would dress as quickly as she could and catch Brad before he went home or ran off to lead one of his meetings. She would make him listen to what she had to say. She had to end this terrible misunderstanding.

Brenda clanged open her locker and tried to pull on her black tights. Her legs were still wet, and the thin nylon fought her as it bunched up around her feet. Her sopping hair was dripping down her back, but she quickly pulled on her skirt and vest, threw her lace scarf around her neck, and stuck her arms into her jean jacket.

Brenda's wet hair slapped her shoulders as she ran across the quad and into the main corridor.

151

She slowed to a careful walk as she passed several open classroom doors.

Brenda knew Brad had trigonometry seventh period and that his class was on the second floor. She was determined to find him. Trying to look as if she had a good reason to be roaming the halls, Brenda glanced in the window of each classroom. The third room she looked into was filled with seniors and she spotted Brad sitting in the far desk of the front row. He was leaning on his arms, his expression preoccupied and tense.

The bell rang and Brenda waited for Brad to come out. When he saw her, his face turned hard, and he rushed ahead of her. Brenda knew that she would have to pursue him if she wanted to settle matters. Fighting her way through the crowded hall, she finally caught up with him.

She stood next to Brad at his locker while he threw a book in. He tossed it much harder than necessary and it bounced off the back of the wall and onto the hallway floor. With increased frustration, Brad picked up the book and threw it in again. When he slammed the door shut, it rang out even over the incredible din of the crowded hallway.

Brad clenched his notebook against his chest and barged down the hall. "Brad, we have to talk," Brenda called after him, trying to cut him off before he turned into the stairwell. He stopped.

"What is there to say?"

Brenda wanted to scream, to shake him. He was making everything so much worse than it had to be. He was being so incredibly unfair.

"Will you let me explain?"

"I have a senior planning meeting," he told her.

"I don't care," Brenda challenged. "This is more important."

Brad looked a little startled at her forcefulness. He paused and walked stiffly into the nearest empty classroom. Brenda followed and closed the door.

"I know what you think about me and Tony," she stated.

"Yeah." Brad leaned back against the blackboard with his arms folded. "What do I think?"

Brenda faced him head on. "You think that just because he hugged me there's something between us."

"Isn't that what a hug usually means?"

"No. Can't a friend hug me without you taking it to mean something romantic is going on?"

"Wait a minute. First you write that love letter to him for the paper —"

"I told you, printing that was Chris's idea."

"Chris didn't write it!"

Brenda stopped. How could she explain anything if Brad refused to listen? Brad was acting as if he was being guided by an automatic pilot, one that was intent on crashing their whole relationship.

"Tony and I are just friends," Brenda repeated.

"Sure," Brad answered sarcastically. "That's why he calls you his favorite girl." Brad started for the door.

Brenda ran in front of him and put her arms out as if to stop a runaway truck.

"All right!" Brenda finally exploded. "You want to think that way about Tony, go ahead. But just remember one thing. I'm not Phoebe! Just because she ran off with somebody else doesn't mean I'm going to. And if you won't believe in me, then it's your problem, not mine!"

For a moment Brad just stared at her, and Brenda thought that maybe he was going to calm down so they could really discuss this problem, figure it out. But no. Brad spun around in a furious huff, swung open the door, and stormed away. As the door slammed behind him, Brenda slunk down at a desk in the empty classroom.

Brenda pounded her fist once on the desktop. Brad's behavior was maddening! He wasn't even giving her a chance. It was like —

Brenda gasped as she realized what it was like. Now she finally knew. She finally knew how Chris, her parents, and the kids at school who had tried to be her friend all felt. You could do only so much if the other person refused to cooperate, if the other person ran every time something went wrong.

Brenda sat down and pressed her cheek on the cool desktop. At first she had thought the problem between Brad and her was that they were too different. Now she knew the problem was they were too much alike.

Chapter
18

Brenda immediately headed for home. She strode down Rose Hill Avenue until she turned onto her street and up the slight hill to her house. She opened the front door, passed through the brick hallway, and ran up the shiny wooden stairs. She dropped her books in the hall and knocked on Chris's door.

"Chris. It's me."

"Come in," her stepsister responded instantly. Brenda opened Chris's door and entered.

Chris was sitting cross-legged on the floor, an algebra book and paper before her. Her silky hair lay neatly against her blue polo shirt. As Brenda walked in, Chris quickly put her homework aside.

"Hi," Chris said with a defensive air. She smiled, but Brenda's stern expression dulled any attempt to lighten the atmosphere. "Sasha just called. She told me you were kind of — um — upset about the article."

Brenda nodded. "Yes."

Chris looked down. "I'm sorry. I know I should have asked you, but I knew that you'd just —"

"Say no?"

Chris looked up with uncertain eyes. "Yes. That's how it's been —" Chris sprang up and guarded her doorway as if she was expecting Brenda to race out. Her blue eyes widened as Brenda purposefully stepped into the center of the room and sat down in the middle of the floor.

Brenda put her arms around her knees and leaned against Chris's bed. Chris was still looking at her with a shocked expression.

"Chris, I know that it hasn't been easy having me in your family," Brenda began slowly. Chris knelt down next to her and sat very still with her hands folded in her lap. "I know that you're trying to help me and that I run away every time things go wrong," Brenda continued.

Brenda paused for a breath and pulled a hunk of fuzz from the thick carpet. "But I'm trying to change that. And in some ways you are just as unfair to me as I am to you."

Chris began nervously to twist a piece of hair around her finger. "I'm sorry. But honest, Bren, everybody thought it was so good. Kids at school today were all talking about how talented you are. What's bad about that?"

Brenda looked hard at her sister. "Brad read it and he thought it meant I was in love with Tony. So things between us may be all over."

Chris closed her eyes and put her hand to her forehead. When she lifted her face again, all the color was drained from her cheeks. "Oh no," she sighed. "Didn't you tell him the truth?"

"I tried, but he wouldn't listen."

"Oh, Brenda, I never would have done it if I'd known that was going to happen."

"Chris, what happened with Brad isn't the important thing right now. What matters is that you respect me enough to find out what I think before you plan out my life."

"I can't believe that Brad thought that." Chris reached for the phone. "I'll call him and explain."

"No, Chris! Not this time. For once, let me handle things in my own way."

Chris slumped down and was silent for a moment. When she raised her head again, Brenda saw the tears forming in her stepsister's eyes. "I would have loved having my essay in the paper," she said softly.

"That's just it! You assume that I have to be just like you. I'm not! Why don't you respect who I am?"

"I do," Chris answered defensively.

"How can you say that when all you do is try to make me into a Chris clone? I'm not Chris Austin and I never will be! But I'm somebody else who's just as worthwhile!"

The two girls stared at each other. Brenda knew that this time she had to stick it out, no matter how difficult or painful. This time she really had to make Chris understand who Brenda was and what she wanted. They couldn't afford any more misunderstandings.

Chris lifted her hands to her face. "I'm so

sorry," she said, the last word sticking in her throat. With a rasping breath, Chris began to cry. For a moment, Brenda watched her sister weep.

But then Brenda felt a tug within herself. She moved toward Chris and tentatively put her arms around her sister. When she felt Chris begin to cry even harder, Brenda tightened her arms in a full hug.

"I know how awful I can be. I'm sorry, too." Brenda patted Chris's back as her sister continued to cry.

They sat together on the floor holding each other for several minutes. As she stroked Chris's back, Brenda realized that in the year the two of them had been members of the same family, this was the first time they had ever shared any affection. Brenda suddenly felt her own eyes well up, and there was no holding back. The pressure exploded at the back of her throat, and the tears flowed. She felt Chris increase her own grip and offer comfort to her.

Finally both girls grew calm; Chris sniffed and broke away. She dragged a box of tissues from her headboard and put it between them. "Want one?" she said with an embarrassed smile.

Brenda nodded and returned Chris's smile. They both blew their noses.

"Brenda," Chris said as she wiped her eyes with the back of her hand, "it's so dumb. Here we are sisters, and I feel like this is the first time we've really talked."

"I know."

"I guess it's been hard for you. I forget that you

had to come to a new place where you didn't know anybody. For me the only new thing has been you and Catherine. But I guess it was wrong to try to push you in with my friends."

"It's not them. I like your friends. It's just —" Brenda suddenly smiled. "How about if I took you to meet some of my friends sometime?"

"What do you mean?"

"Why don't you come down to Garfield House one day after school, see what I do there."

Chris responded immediately. "I'd like that."

Brenda looked at her sister's searching eyes and knew she was on the right track. There was a reward for not running, for having the guts to stay and talk things out. For the first time, Brenda felt like Chris's equal.

"How about tomorrow after school, if you don't have honor society or something?"

Chris smiled. "I do, but I'll just stay for a half hour or so and then meet you down there."

"Okay."

There was an awkward pause. Both girls smiled shyly. Brenda got up and started to walk toward the door.

"Bren."

"Yes?"

"What about Brad? What are you going to do?"

Brenda stopped. What was she going to do? Yes, she liked him — maybe even loved him — but he had turned his back on her. She couldn't retreat to that angry place where the only release was to run away. If that's where Brad wanted to be, he would have to go alone. If he really didn't believe in her, then their relationship was over.

"I guess I'll write him a letter and tell him the truth. After that it's up to him."

Chris nodded sadly. "It's all my fault. If I hadn't given that article to the paper. . . ."

"Maybe it was a good thing. Maybe Brad and I didn't belong together after all."

Chris shook her head sadly. "I don't think anything good came out of putting your essay in that dumb paper. I'm so sorry."

"It's okay," Brenda said quietly. "We'll just wait and see what happens."

As she sat in the empty journalism room hashing over the mysteries of account books, Sasha Jenkins felt as if she'd descended into permanent confusion. Somehow the Roy Rogers had gotten a full-page ad when they had only paid for a quarter, and Rezato boutique had only gotten a quarter-page when they'd paid for a full. The only thing Sasha knew for sure was that the whole mess was giving her a headache.

Piercing a pencil through the base of her thick ponytail, Sasha surveyed the account book again. Chuck Couch, who usually took care of the advertising records, would pick this week to get the flu. Sasha glanced at Chuck's empty desk and thought about all those Doritos he wolfed down after school every day. No wonder he was sick. She pushed up the sleeves of her Indian cotton blouse and released a sigh of frustration.

"Oh, Lord!" she heaved.

"You called?" boomed back an arrogant voice from just outside the doorway.

Sasha cringed. John Marquette's head was just visible around the edge of the doorway. Somehow she knew the rest of him was not far behind. Sure enough, he laughed and lumbered toward her.

He had obviously just come from wrestling practice, his dark hair was wet and his cheeks still glistened with triumph. Where were his eyes? Sasha thought to herself. Everything about Marquette was so large and overbearing, except for his eyes. They were like two pinholes in his big, beefy face.

"Hi, you little fox, you," he swaggered, plopping his thick frame onto the top of her desk.

There was something different about Marquette this time and it made Sasha uneasy. Since the ski trip he'd shown an edge of defensiveness every time she'd seen him. But today he was relaxed. Marquette looked confident and ready to go in for the kill. It made Sasha a little nervous.

She pushed back her chair and stood up. "I'm not a fox, or a little fox, or a foxette. I'm a woman. And I'm going home now. Bye."

Sasha pulled her sweater off the back of her chair. When she bent down to get her backpack Marquette moved in. He came up close behind her, wrapping his arms around her tiny waist. She stood up suddenly and managed to push him back with her elbow and throw him off balance. He laughed lustily.

"Hey, foxette, I think you're going to have to start being a little nicer to me."

"Am I?"

He grinned. "You sure are. You see, you owe me one."

"What do I owe you?"

"Plenty, foxette, plenty. See, my cousin was expecting to get his paper yesterday — you know, like he always does. And see, he was especially waiting for it because my picture was in it."

"So?" Sasha had no idea what he was driving at.

"So we never got our paper. I had to steal one out of the newspaper office this morning. My cousin is ticked off about it. He's really ticked."

Sasha remembered Janie saying something about Superjock, but in the confusion with the advertising she had not paid attention.

"Superjock didn't get a paper yesterday?"

"No, foxette, absolutely not."

Sasha bit the inside of her cheek.

"So, that sounds like a royal goof up on your part to me," Marquette swaggered. "I'd say my cousin has good reason to complain, wouldn't you agree?"

Sasha felt a little weak. "I guess."

"So, the only way I can see for you to keep Superjock's business is. . . ."

Sasha swallowed her pride. "To do an interview with you, John."

"You got it."

Sasha knew she had lost. She did owe Marquette one. But somehow she would make the best of it. She thought fast. One thing she was confident of with Marquette, she would always be way ahead of him in a thinking contest.

"Okay, I'll do an interview with you. Tell your cousin I'm sorry about the mix-up."

Marquette broke into a big smile. Now his eyes were completely invisible. "I'll do that."

162

Sasha's mind raced ahead. Maybe something could really be gained out of this. If she approached the interview in the right way, she might be able to wangle some choice info out of Marquette. Sasha had heard that certain athletes were getting breaks on grades so they could continue to play. Marquette might just be dumb enough to give her some scoops.

She tossed her backpack over her shoulder and started to walk out. Marquette stuck by her.

"There's one more thing, foxette," he said bluntly.

"What?"

Marquette suddenly stopped and blocked her way with his strong body. "This interview. We're going to do it somewhere nice and private" — he laughed — "where we can really talk."

Fine, thought Sasha. She knew that Marquette was still trying to prove himself to her, but she could handle him. No guy had succeeded in scaring her yet, and John Marquette was not about to be the first. Whatever he tried, she would outsmart him. As she rushed away down the hall, Sasha felt calmer and more confident. She could handle John Marquette any day.

As Marquette watched Sasha hurry down the hallway, he leered and rubbed his hands together.

"Woo, this should be good," he said in a low, menacing voice as he turned away.

There was one thing John Marquette was sure of: No girl had outsmarted him yet.

Chapter
19

Brenda stopped in the middle of the quad and pulled the hood of her yellow rain slicker over her head. The air was misty and thick, so gray it looked like rain, although not a drop was actually coming down. The grass was spongy, and small pools of muddy water formed each time she took a step.

Reaching into her pocket, Brenda felt the sharp corner of the envelope. School had ended ten minutes before, and she was on her way to deliver her letter to Brad. After he read it, he would have time to think things over while she went down to Garfield House to meet Chris. Later in the evening she would call Brad — if he would talk to her — and see if he had changed his mind. She was turning toward the main building when she thought she heard someone call her from behind.

"I read your article in *The Red and the Gold*. It was really good."

For a second Brenda wasn't sure if the voice was aimed at her or not. The tone was so breathy and thin. The touch on her arm was equally light and tentative.

Janie Barstow stood next to her, holding her notebook tight against her chest. They had sat next to each other in art class the semester before, although Janie had been too timid and Brenda too sullen to ever strike up a conversation. Janie looked nervous about approaching Brenda but managed to smile.

"Thanks," Brenda said.

"Are you going to write any more?" Janie asked shyly.

Brenda looked at the damp grass and didn't answer.

"I don't know," Brenda said finally. "I'm glad you liked it, though."

Janie brushed back her bangs and smiled. "I thought it was great. I hope you write some more if you feel like it."

"Thanks."

Janie waved tentatively and walked away. Brenda watched her leaving and called out just before she was out of sight. "Bye, Janie. I really appreciate your telling me."

Janie turned slowly back, smiled sweetly, and waved again. Brenda sighed at the irony of it. Janie was not the only student that had come up to her that day to compliment her on the essay. The article, which had caused her so much trouble, was also the source of the first positive attention she'd ever earned at Kennedy.

Brenda leaned her head to one side and stuck

her hands in her pockets. She wished Brad could see it the way Janie did. Brenda understood the power of jealousy — look at the way she had reacted to having Chris as a sister. But what Brad was doing was beyond plain jealousy. He was so comfortable with his anger that he was refusing to take it off.

The edge of the letter brushed against Brenda's hand. She had to deliver it in time to get downtown and meet Chris at Garfield House. There was no more delaying it. She crossed the quad, then went inside the main building and down two halls towards the council room.

Brenda took the envelope out of her pocket and grasped it firmly. She was just about to round the last corner when she saw a shadow at the other end of the hallway. Instinctively she looked to see if someone was there. The shadow had disappeared, but now she thought she heard a voice: a muffled, low voice broken by long moments of quiet. Brenda slowly moved closer.

As soon as she saw the slope of his wide shoulders, Brenda knew it was Brad. There was no mistaking his tall frame, his starched shirt, the way the back of his straight hair just rested over his collar. He was in a nook at the end of the hall, a small foyer that led into the chemistry labs. Just seeing him made her skin feel feathery and hot.

Brenda held out her letter and quietly walked closer. Her heart started tapping like a tiny snare drum. But when Brenda took another step the tapping stopped and her insides went dead. Brad was not alone; he was with Phoebe.

It was like being in a dream — a nightmare —

166

and Brenda stood helplessly and watched. Brad still had his back to her, but there was no mistaking when he leaned in and took Phoebe in his arms. Phoebe's hair spilled over his sleeve, bright and colorful against his pale blue shirt. What was hardest to watch was the naturalness, the ease with which they held each other. They were whispering, but Brenda could only make out a few sounds. Phoebe was trying to explain something, one hand gesturing close to her body. Brad was comforting her, moving his head in slow, deliberate nods.

Finally Phoebe lifted her face out of the crook of Brad's arm and looked at Brenda. For a prolonged moment, the girls locked eyes. Brenda felt like a deer in the headlights. She was unable to move. She tried to smile, to send Phoebe the message, "You win," but the muscles in her face would not respond. Brenda knew it was over — there was no more doubt about that. The slightest hope had just flickered out. She was on her own.

Without saying anything, Brenda slipped off in the other direction and out of the metal double doors toward the front of the school. Once down the main corridor she was outside again. The chilled, moist air stung her face.

Brenda began to race across the parking lot, but she stopped herself. She was not going to run anywhere. Instead, she walked slowly and tried to think. She went over to a large trash barrel and held Brad's letter over it. Tearing the paper into tiny pieces, she watched while each one floated to the soggy bottom of the can.

After she had dropped the last shred and

watched it drift down, she pressed her eyes shut. She tried to erase the vision of Brad and Phoebe from her mind, but it was burned there. She knew the only thing she could do was accept it, and wait for the pain to fade. For the moment, something was grabbing at her insides. Brenda wrapped her arms around herself and started to cry.

She didn't even bother to hide her face. She didn't care if someone saw her. She *wanted* someone to see her, to come over and ask if she was all right. Brenda wished Janie Barstow would come back and search the parking lot for her. But Janie wasn't there. Brenda recalled she was supposed to meet Chris at Garfield House, and for the very first time she was glad that she had her stepsister. Chris would comfort her. Chris would understand.

Brenda let her tears stream down her face as she walked to the bus stop. She wiped them away with the cuff of her jacket, but fresh ones replaced the old. Eventually she didn't even bother to brush the wetness away. She just let it flow until she tasted salt and her whole face grew sensitive and tired.

There was no one else at the stop. As Brenda boarded the bus, the driver smiled sympathetically. She sat down halfway back and pressed a chapped cheek against the window. Gazing out at the street she watched the familiar colonial shops of Rose Hill fade into the busier, more congested streets of Washington, D.C.

As the bus pulled closer to the center of Georgetown, Brenda found herself twisting in her seat and looking behind her. In spite of her distress, this was one of the first times that she did not feel as if she was fleeing from some terrible unin-habitable place in order to seek refuge at Garfield House. This time she felt that going to visit people that she cared about — and she was glad her sister, Chris, would be there.

By the time she walked to Garfield House, Brenda had stopped crying. She felt limp and lonely, but also cleansed and free. Her legs felt slightly weak as she lowered herself onto Gar-field's front stoop. She sat with her face resting in her hands, patting her cheeks with the arm of her jacket. With a sigh and a slight shiver, Brenda studied the townhouses across the street and waited for Chris.

Brenda was so happy to see Chris's blond hair and erect posture coming up the walkway that she didn't notice anything else. Immediately she stood and hugged her stepsister. Chris returned her hug, but quickly released her hold to look Brenda in the face. She smoothed Brenda's damp hair away from her eyes and spoke very fast.

"Bren, I'm not trying to interfere in your life, I swear, but he wanted to find you and I knew where you were so I hope it's okay that —"

Brenda raised her eyes and looked over Chris's shoulder. Standing right behind her stepsister, his brown eyes brimming with tears, was Brad.

Chapter
20

"I think I'll go inside," Chris said, opening the front door of Garfield House.

Brenda couldn't take her eyes from Brad.

"Tony's expecting you. He wants to show you around," she told her stepsister. Brenda felt Chris pat her lightly on the shoulder, then heard the door swing shut. Brenda and Brad were alone. There was a long, difficult silence as they sat side by side on the front stoop.

Brenda looked ahead. "Hello," she said slowly.

"Hi." Brad cleared his throat. "I'm glad I ran into Chris at school. I wouldn't have known where to find you."

"From what I saw, you weren't thinking too much about finding me."

He reached over and lightly touched her hand. "Hear what I have to say, Bren. Don't be a jerk like me."

Brenda put her head down. "Okay."

"I know you saw me and Phoebe in the hall."

Brenda couldn't help looking up. "How did you know? You didn't notice me."

"Phoebe told me."

Brenda bit her lip. It was hard to hear Brad say Phoebe's name. She laced her fingers together and clenched her hands.

"I think I understand now what you were saying before — about Tony just being your friend and hugging him and all." Brad's words came out slow and careful.

"Why do you say that?"

"Because that's how I felt this afternoon."

"What do you mean?"

"With Phoebe. See, she came up to me after school and wanted to talk about getting back together."

"And so you —"

"So I said no. I don't want to get back together. Because it's over between the two of us, and because of how I feel about you."

Brenda shifted. Her hands began to relax.

"So after I told Phoebe that it was all over, she started to cry, and I hugged her because I wanted to make her feel better. I care about her." Brad paused. "As a friend."

"Are you sure that's all you feel for Phoebe?"

Brad looked at her firmly. "I'm positive. I think I was really over her a while ago, I just hung onto to being mad for some reason."

He paused and ran his hand through his hair. "Phoebe told me that she's been acting pretty weird to you. She feels bad about it. I guess since Griffin broke up with her, and she's been going through a rough time."

For a moment they were both quiet. Brenda leaned forward. "At least Phoebe told you that she saw me in the hall," she offered.

"Yeah. Do you believe me? I swear, it's the truth."

"Yes, I believe you," Brenda answered cautiously. Brad started to move closer, but he stopped when he met Brenda's eyes.

"Why didn't you believe me when I told you there was nothing between me and Tony?" she demanded. "I could understand how you felt when you saw him hug me, but why wouldn't you listen to me afterwards? How can we be together if we can't talk to each other?"

"I'm sorry. This jerky guy teased me about your article and I got so mad. I was just being macho and stupid."

"Somebody teased you about me?"

"Yeah. John Marquette. The lowest form of human being. I almost killed him."

"Brad!"

"Actually I didn't almost kill him. The teacher stopped it before anything happened. It's a good thing, because Marquette is huge. He probably would have killed me." Brad tentatively leaned his head on her shoulder. "You wouldn't have liked that . . ." he looked up at her, ". . . would you?"

"It's a good thing you didn't ask me an hour ago." Brenda couldn't help cracking a tiny smile.

Brad turned to face her and took hold of her shoulders.

"Brenda, I'm sorry. I know I acted like a jerk about Tony. I guess I've been so mad about everything the last couple of months that I forgot how not to be mad."

"It's time to remember. That goes for both of us."

"Okay." Brad gently touched the side of her face. "So, what do you think? Are you willing to try again? Brenda and Brad, take three. Do you...."

Before he could finish, Brenda leaned close to him, folded her arms around his neck, and kissed him. Once she found his familiar warmth, she knew it was the right thing to do. Brad's arms flew around her, and he held her so tightly that it almost hurt.

"I love you," she heard him whisper. "I don't ever want us to go through anything like this again. I'm sorry."

"I love you, too," Brenda answered, kissing him again. She rested her head against him, feeling the wonderful softness of his neck against her cheek. Finally they relaxed with their arms around each other's shoulders.

"I was so mad when I saw that article," Brad laughed. "Sasha told me what happened. The whole thing was pretty nuts."

"I was pretty mad, too, you know. Think of me, sitting in Barnes's class opening that paper up and seeing —"

At that moment the door opened and Chris stuck her head out.

"Hi." Chris grinned. "Is the coast clear? Can we join you?"

Brad and Brenda laughed. It was very obvious that they had resolved matters and their romance was on again. Chris grinned and stepped onto the stoop. She hesitated long enough to hold the door open, and Tony Martinez followed. Brad immediately rose.

He extended his hand to Tony. "Hi. Sorry I wasn't very friendly when you came to school. It was a misunderstanding."

Tony shook his hand gratefully and slapped Brad on the side of the arm. "No problem."

"I hope we helped Garfield. All the council members are getting info out to the whole school."

"Great." Tony smiled and put his hands on his hips. "Hey, Brenda," he winked.

"What's up, Ton?" Brenda leaned her head back to look up at her friend.

"I just saw this."

Tony shot her a coy look and pulled a folded copy of her newspaper article out of his jeans pocket.

Brenda laughed and put her head in her hands. "Oh no, that dumb article is going to follow me everywhere. I can't stand it."

Tony opened his eyes wide. "Why do you say it's dumb? I liked it. Nobody every wrote about me before. I was going to ask you for a bunch more copies."

They all laughed. Tony crouched down and sat next to Brenda.

"Listen to me, my favorite girl," he teased, his muscular arms folded over his chest. "Don't put this piece of writing down." He waved the clipping and stuck it back in his pocket. "First, because you wrote it. Second —" he grinned at Chris and Brad "— because it's about me. And third —"

"Yes, Tony," Brenda laughed.

"Third because a girl named Julie Meeker just happened to get a hold of this somewhere in Georgetown yesterday, and because of it she should be off the streets and into Garfield House tonight."

Brenda stood up slowly. She looked from Tony to Chris to Brad. They were all beaming; Chris was hopping from foot to foot. But Brenda knew none of them felt as good as she did.

"Are you serious? Julie Meeker found out about Garfield from my dumb article?"

"That's right." Tony nodded. "So maybe it's not so dumb, huh?"

"Maybe not," Brenda whispered with a glance at Chris. Brad reached over and took her hands. He was gazing at her with the most wonderful expression. Brenda threw back her head and laughed a throaty laugh. "Maybe it wasn't so dumb at all."

Chapter
21

"Woody, put me down!"

Woody Webster was straining and turning red as he heroically held onto Sasha Jenkins in the middle of the Rose Hill Sub Shop. He had both arms wrapped around Sasha's waist and had elevated her all of six inches above the floor. One of his suspender clips had just popped off the waistband of his jeans.

"I'm not putting you down yet, little foxette," Woody said in a mock deep voice. "Not yet, honey. John Marquette doesn't put any girl down until he gets exactly what he wants out of her."

Sasha giggled, but then tried to keep from laughing. She slugged Woody repeatedly in the chest. "That is the worst impression I have ever seen and it's not funny, so put me down!"

"I don't know," Ted shouted from the table. "I think it's the best thing I've seen Woody do since he dressed up like a refrigerator for Halloween."

176

"Don't encourage him," Sasha countered. "Some days, Webster, you're impossible."

"I'm not Webster!" Woody protested. "I'm Marquette, and I'm doing this for your own good."

Woody finally put Sasha down. "Okay. Don't say I didn't warn you. If you think Marquette just wants an interview out of you, you're crazy. That guy's the biggest lech in the world."

Sasha sat back down at the table with Ted, Peter, and Woody. She should have known better than to come to the Sub in the exclusive company of the guys. She needed Chris and Phoebe to protect her. She had told the guys what happened in the newspaper office, and they wouldn't let the conversation drop.

"Look," Sasha protested, "I can handle him. He's just a jock."

"Sure, he's just a jock," Peter responded while he folded his bomber jacket over the bench. "Like a redwood's just a tree. I hate to agree with Woody and Ted, but for once I think they're not being overly cautious. Man, there's one word for Marquette — animal."

"That's right," Ted agreed.

The girl at the counter finally called their numbers, to Sasha's relief. Ted went to pick up the food — a giant sub for the guys and one veggie-cheese deluxe for Sasha, three Cokes and one water. Sasha turned up her nose as the boys plunged their straws into the fizzy stuff.

"Where's everybody else?" Woody finally spoke after the first three or four bites. "Seems like we're always missing somebody."

177

"Chris went somewhere to meet Brenda," Ted announced.

"And Pheeberooni's home doing the mope," Woody added. "I have to do something about that. I hope it doesn't last through Christmas vacation."

"What you want to do may not solve Phoebe's problem," Ted teased, referring to Woody's long-time affection for Phoebe.

"Don't remind me," Woody huffed, taking another huge bite of his sandwich.

"I think Phoebe might really be upset because Brad and Brenda got together," Sasha offered.

"Nah," Peter waved his hand. "Why should she care? She gave Brad the royal dump."

"You don't know women," Sasha lectured. "Just because a girl breaks up with a guy doesn't mean that she wants somebody else to walk in and take him."

"Sounds fair," commented Ted.

"Well, it's true. You guys just don't understand how it works." Sasha lifted her sub, trying not to eat her long hair along with it.

"Anyway," Ted added, "I think Brad and Brenda may already be a thing of the past. When I asked him how she was after school, I thought he was going to tie me to a post."

Sasha picked the pickles from her sandwich and neatly lined them up on a napkin. "It's all my fault. I never should have put that thing in the paper without asking. I didn't know it would wreck everything between them."

"But, Sash," Peter kidded, "I thought you knew everything about women."

"I do." She frowned. "It's guys I can't always figure out."

They went back to their subs, and Sasha and Woody were having a tug-of-war over one small piece of green pepper. Just then the door to the shop opened, and Sasha dropped her end of the pepper.

Ted stood up and smiled. "Chris! Hey." His girl friend greeted him with a hug, sat down on his lap, and gave him another quick hug.

"How are things going?" Ted asked.

"Great." She beamed. "There's a couple of other people coming. They're just parking the car, so you've got to make room."

The crowd immediately spread out around the long table.

"Okay." Woody nodded. "The more the. . . ."

"Shhhh." Sasha motioned to Woody. "Look!"

They all turned around. Brad was just opening the heavy door as Brenda slipped in next to him. She looked over at the table and offered a tentative, nervous smile.

"Hi, everybody," Brad said as he approached the table. Ted got up and slapped him on the back.

Brenda shyly stood behind Brad. Sasha cleared a place across from her and smiled at both of them.

"Hi," Brenda said, sliding onto the bench between Brad and Chris. Sasha immediately leaned across the table and touched Brenda's hand.

"Brenda, I apologize about the newspaper. Are you still mad at me?"

Brenda looked to Brad, lingering an extra moment to enjoy the warmth in his eyes. She turned back to Sasha. "It's okay, Sasha. It ended up working out just fine."

Janie Barstow was wandering across the parking lot of the Mill Creek Shopping Center as Brad and Brenda approached the old timbered door of the Sub Shop. She waited until the couple was inside before following and peeking in one of the shop's large glass windows. Holding the door open a few inches, Janie felt a bubble form in her throat when she spotted Peter. He was laughing, saying something to Brad across the table. Soon they were all giggling, and Janie thought it would be wonderful to have a group of friends like that.

Janie turned away and crossed the parking lot. The tinkle of bells sounded across the mall. Christmas decorations hung everywhere.

Janie wrapped her scarf around her neck and waited on the corner for her mom to pick her up. They were going downtown so that Janie could try on new clothes — a task Janie considered one of the all-time terrible ordeals. Even worse, Janie knew that her mother was going to ask her how the newspaper was going and what Janie was going to volunteer for next.

Janie thought about the before and after pictures in fashion magazines. That's what she wished would happen to her. Every night she went to bed and wished that when she woke up she'd be somebody else. Deep within herself was a smart and caring and interesting girl. Janie pulled her collar up around her neck as she wondered if that person ever would emerge.

Janie looked up. A big round man in a red suit and pointy cap was walking toward her. He was getting wet, and he still hadn't put on his beard, and there was a silly grin on his face. He was headed for the big toy store, but even though she tried to ignore him Janie could tell that the Santa Claus was going to approach her. As he came closer, Janie backed under the eaves of the drugstore and leaned against the wall. Santa snuck up right next to her.

"Merry Christmas," he said with a genuine smile.

"Ho, ho,ho," Janie answered in the flattest possible voice.

Santa leaned back against the wall and pulled his beard out of his pocket. "It can't be that bad," he joked as he pulled the thin elastic straps over his ears.

Janie shrugged and looked into the street for her mother's car.

"Is my beard on straight?" Santa asked.

Janie turned to face him. He was an older man with kind gray eyes, a bulbous nose, and a fake beard that was bunched on one side of his face.

"It's not straight at all," she confessed.

He twisted up his face and tried to fix the beard, but he was only making it worse.

"Here, I'll do it." Janie reached up and adjusted the beard.

"Ho, ho, ho," Santa boomed with an uninhibited laugh.

His gusto was infectious, and Janie had to smile. "Ho, ho, ho," she echoed, this time with a little more feeling.

"Good. Now what can I bring you for Christmas, young lady?" Santa Claus asked her.

Janie looked down at her feet, her shyness returning. If only Christmas really worked that way. If only she could get what she really *did* want.

"I don't know," Janie said quietly.

Santa Claus smiled and shrugged. "Well, if you figure it out, come by the toy store and let me know."

"Okay."

The Santa Claus waddled off and Janie walked back to the corner. She couldn't stop thinking about the happy group sitting so close by in the Sub Shop. Chris looked so content sitting on Ted's lap. Brenda Austin had changed completely from the quiet, intimidating girl who sat next to Janie in art class.

Janie knew what she wanted, but she would have felt silly saying it out loud to Santa Claus. She would have felt silly telling anyone.

"A brand-new Janie," she whispered to herself. "That's what I want — a brand-new Janie."

Coming Soon...
Couples #4
Made For Each Other

Janie tapped gently, then waited. Nothing happened. Taking a deep breath, she rapped hard three times. But the door remained closed.

She was turning away again when she thought she heard a slight rustling noise inside the room. She had a sudden image of Henry standing by the door, holding his breath, and listening. The loud knocking must have startled him. He probably was waiting for some teacher or one of the watchmen to discover him.

She put her head next to the door and said in a low voice, "Henry, are you in there? It's me, Janie Barstow."

No answer. "I was here yesterday," she added. But there was still no answer. She felt like a total fool, standing there in the hallway talking to a closed door. It was no use; he wasn't there. But she couldn't leave without taking one last shot.

"Let me in, Henry," she said, slightly louder. "I have something of yours."

The lock clicked and the door opened a crack. One eye looked at her for a moment, then Henry opened the door wide. "Quick," he said. "I don't want anybody to see us."

She slipped through and he locked the door behind her.

He reached for the portfolio and she placed it in his hand. The intensity of the relief on his face as he glanced inside was almost embarrassing to see. His intensity both disturbed and attracted her. It was as if she had unknowingly broken something important to him and now he was expecting her to make it whole again.

"I'd better go now," Janie said. "Would you mind unlocking the door?"

Join the Team!

They're talented. They're fabulous-looking. They're winners! And they've got what you want! Don't miss any of these exciting CHEERLEADERS books!